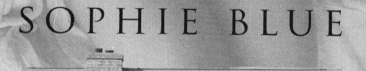

The
Best Friend's
SISTER

SOPHIE BLUE

Cover Design by LJ Designs
Editing by Magnolia Author Services
Proofreading by Gem's Precise Proofreads

This book is a work of fiction. Names, characters and places, and incidents are either the product of the author's imagination or used fictitiously.

For Alex
Our random chats and ridiculous puns
never fail to make me smile.
Thank you for pushing me to finish this
one. Here's to coconut lattes with a shot of
salted caramel.

PROLOGUE

Charlotte

Breaking up always sucks. But finding out that your relationship is over when you watch your boyfriend proposing to someone else on live stream over social media...

Yeah, that really sucks.

Carl and I weren't the perfect couple by any means, but I didn't deserve that. After his surprise public service announcement, I found out after that not only is he a cheating arsehole, but he'd been leading a double life. He'd had another girlfriend for the past six months of our two-year relationship. Something he didn't think was worth mentioning to me, apparently. Funny because she knew and wasn't bothered by it. Carl had told her it was all but over and he was just hanging on until the car was paid off by our joint loan.

What an arsehole.

Logically, I know I am better off without him. I know he is the lowest of the low to do that to someone, and that I had a lucky escape. But the humiliation that came with him doing it so publicly would take some getting over. People looked at me with pity and it made me sick to my stomach. The video had gone viral. People tagged me, saying he was my boyfriend and had proposed to someone else. Asking if I knew, how I felt, if I'd suspected it.

Not only was it mortifying, being the town's joke, but I felt my heart shatter into thousands of jagged shards every time I was reminded of his betrayal. It was my life; he was who I thought I'd spend forever with. Our relationship meant something to me. I thought it meant something to him too. How does someone do that to another person? String them along while they play house with another woman? Every time I think about it, I feel both nauseous and livid. How dare he!

Angry and betrayed doesn't even begin to describe the myriad of emotions constantly battling it out inside me. Add in how I feel like a joke every time I hear all the whispers, see all the looks of pity from friends and strangers. I need to get away from it all! But how?

That's the problem with social media. Once something

is out there, it's out there forever.

CHAPTER ONE

Charlotte

W hat does anyone do when their life goes to hell? Move back in with their parents, of course. So here I am on a Saturday night, sitting in my parents' cosy living room playing our favourite card game, gin.

Discarding one card, I pick up another and slot the five of hearts next to the other two fives I'm holding. It's Dad's turn and he spends ages thinking about his next move. His salt and pepper coloured eyebrows scrunching as he overthinks his play. Trying not to roll my eyes out of impatience, I take a sip of my drink.

The familiarity of my parents' house brings me comfort. I've always felt safe here, growing up I didn't have a care in the world. The beige walls are covered in framed prints of my brother and I, family snaps taken over the past twenty odd years. Life was so much simpler back then, not just because social media didn't exist. God, I can't even imagine growing up with it, the thought alone has ice flowing through my veins.

The doorbell rings, pulling me from my thoughts, and I turn to my mum and raise a brow. She didn't say that they were expecting company.

"Hello?" Alex calls from the hallway. Letting out a sigh of relief that I don't have to make small talk with a neighbour, I relax back into the sofa.

Entertaining is the last thing I want to do right now, I think as I glance at my reflection in the mirror above the fireplace. I'm twenty-eight, and I'm drinking strawberry milk from a carton in my polka dot pyjamas. It doesn't get more rock and roll than this. But after my car crash of a break up, I needed familiarity. I needed to be in a safe place surrounded by love.

Smiling, I look up when my big brother walks into the room. Alex is six foot and the complete opposite to me. Where I'm short, blonde and blue-eyed, Alex inherited our Dad's looks. He's tall, dark-haired and brown-eyed. Dressed in a grey suit, with his freshly shaven face, we couldn't be any more different.

"Hey, love, are you ok?" Mum asks, standing to give Alex a hug which he returns with a smile. Her blonde bob sways with the movement.

"Yeah, all good. Just thought I'd stop by on my way home from work and check in on my favourite people." He grins and looks my way.

I try not to grimace because I love my brother, but I hate that people are still offering me sympathy. It's been six weeks and I just want to forget it ever happened. I'm not sending invites out to my pity party. It's a private event.

"We're good," I say, taking another slurp of my strawberry milk and looking over at the TV to see what Dad has put on now.

He's obsessed with antique shows. Maybe he thinks he'll find a treasure in his hoarding shed. Mum is always nagging him to throw stuff out, but he says you'll never know when something may become of use again. While that does make sense, keeping three kettles, just in case, does seem a tad excessive.

"Yeah, looks like it," he says with a scoff, shaking his head and running his fingers through his messy brown locks.

The remark immediately gets my back up. I'm sick of his nagging. He doesn't get it. He can tell me to move on until he's blue in the face, but he just doesn't understand. My whole life has been turned upside down. I can't just shake it off and move on. I need time to grieve for my former life, for the hopes and dreams I had for my future with Carl.

"What's that supposed to mean?" I ask as I stand, with my hands finding my hips defensively as my blood pumps through me. The sound of it is deafening in my ears, and I wonder if they can hear it.

Ok, so he doesn't want an invite to my pity party, great.

But if he thinks he can judge me, he's got another thing coming. I get enough crap from the outside world. I'll be damned if I'm letting my family get in on the action.

"You're spending Saturday night at your parents' in your PJs drinking strawberry milk. It's not even nine o'clock, Lottie," Alex points out.

So what? How dare he judge me.

"I live here, in case you forgot. And I'll drink strawberry milk whenever I damn well please!"

I know I'm being petulant, but I don't need him shaming me. I know I'm hiding. But wouldn't you if the whole word had witnessed the public, humiliating demise of your relationship?

"I'm worried about you. I'm not trying to be a dick, I promise." He gives me a cheeky grin and I offer him a small smile back. It's hard to stay mad at my brother. I know he means well. "Anyway, I have a crazy idea that I wanted to run past you."

"Ok?" I say, sitting back on the sofa and looking over at him in curiosity.

I take a loud slurp of my milk in defiance while I wait for him to divulge more information.

"Do you remember Ollie?" he asks, and I nod as his best friend's face flashes into my memory.

"Your mate? From uni? Yeah, of course." They were inseparable when they were at Southampton University. With his dad working away a lot, and the rest of Ollie's family being in the US, we took him under our wing and he spent a lot of time here. He and my brother always had a fan club following them around. Hardly surprising given that

Ollie was sexy as sin. Add in his sinful smile and he had all the local girls swooning, me included.

"Well, I was talking to him yesterday, and he's just moved into his grandparents' old place in the US. He's renovating it, wants to turn it into a B&B. It needs a lot of work. It's the sort of project you dream of, with your obsession for interior design. If you're interested, Ollie would be glad to have your help with it. Think of it as a free holiday!"

"In Alabama?" I ask, surprised. That was unexpected. He wants me to help him renovate a house in the US?

"No, they lived in North Carolina. You said you wanted to get away from here. From everything that happened. Where better than halfway across the world?" Alex smiles and I think about it.

I would be far, far away from all of this crap. It could be a fresh start for me...and I do love interior design. While other kids were playing dress up with their dolls and enjoying picking outfits, I preferred decorating their houses and getting new furniture for them.

"I don't know. I'd need to look into flight prices, getting a visa…" Logic starts to take over, would it even be possible? It wouldn't be cheap, and Carl has pretty much left me high and dry.

"I think you should go, love," my mum pipes up from where she is perched on the arm of Dad's chair, and I look over at her in surprise. Mum's the sort of woman who overthinks everything. Makes a list of pros and cons, and then makes a spreadsheet. She's never been quick to come to a decision and a part of me worries that maybe I have overstayed my welcome.

"You do?" She nods and looks over to where my brother is now leaning against the doorframe. With her platinum blonde hair and kind face, I'm always told we look alike.

"Your brother is right, it's a great excuse for a free holiday. And you need to get away from this, get some space and heal. It's not healthy to be surrounded by all of the memories. Dad and I will pay for your flight and visa." She looks down at Dad and he nods in agreement.

My heart swells at the love in the room, how they're trying to fix me even though I'm no longer sure that's possible. Maybe this is what I need, some time away to collect myself and figure out what I want going forward. It's not like there is much keeping me here now. Other than my family, what have I got to hang around for? My job pays the bills, but it doesn't inspire anything in me. The plan was to save up and take an Open University degree in interior design. But maybe a little real life experience isn't a bad idea. Aren't potential employers also after experience as well as qualifications? The course will always be there, but will an opportunity like this ever present itself again?

Maybe it's time I stop playing safe and take a chance. Looking around the room, I see nothing but love and support and it warms my heart.

"You're right. This will be good for me. When do I leave?"

CHAPTER TWO

Ollie

Taking another mouthful of coffee, I stare out to the sea and wonder where to even begin. I'm out of my depth here. I can't afford to hire people to help transform the house, so I'm doing the majority of the work myself. I just hope I can do it justice. Gram used to say this house was magic. She said the ocean listened to your dreams and washed them right up on the shore to you. *If only.*

Then I'd look over at the waves and see them both riding one onto the beach. Chuckling at the thought of Gram riding a wave like a surfer chick, I put my mug onto the bannister and lean on it, watching the soothing waves.

My chest is heavy, weighed down with the thought that I'm never going to see them again. Sitting here with them and watching as they bickered was something I regret taking for granted. The sun doesn't seem as bright today, and I wonder if it too is mourning the loss of my grandparents.

Standing on the porch of their beach house, I watch as the waves crest and then crash on the shore. There's something about the sea that is so soothing. When I was a kid, Pops and Gram used to take me to the beach all the time when I stayed during the summers. When they passed and left the house to me, I had mixed feelings. I love it here, and North Carolina will always have a piece of my heart. But I can't imagine living here permanently, not without them.

Everywhere I look, I see scenes from the past playing out. Pops and I on the beach, kicking a soccer ball around. Gram walking onto the porch with a plate of baked goods and me running up the stairs, taking them two at a time, to get to her. Pops reading the morning paper and putting the world to rights as Gram sits nearby, shaking her head with a knowing smile. So many memories, so much history. The thought of selling the house never once crossed my mind. It's too special to part with. Which is where the idea of converting it into a bed and breakfast came from. It's a great house for making memories in, so if I won't be living here, why not let other families create their own?

It's old fashioned but in great shape. The stairs from the porch lead right onto the beach. There's nothing better than waking up and feeling the sand beneath your feet while sipping your morning coffee. I do miss certain aspects of being here. Mainly, I miss my grandparents. But now money is tight, thanks to my lousy excuse of an ex, so I need to get this renovated and making money and soon. I can't bear to sell it, not with all the good memories, not with how much Gram and Pops loved it, so I need to start either renting rooms out or renting the house as a whole.

Checking my watch, I see I have around thirty minutes before I have to set off to pick up Charlotte from the airport. Alex and I met in University. I was born and raised in England, my mother was a Brit, my father an American. When Alex and I met, we struck up a bromance instantly. We spent the holidays at his parents' house, it was my home away from home after my parents moved back to the US. His family were always there for me, and his mum still calls me every few weeks to check in and make sure I'm taking care of myself. While I don't make it back to the UK as often as I'd like to, Alex usually comes to visit at least a couple of times a year. If it weren't for his family, I'm sure he would have moved over here.

When he mentioned that his sister was going through some crap because of a bad breakup, I felt for her. My breakup may have been my doing, but my ex didn't exactly leave me much choice. It was pretty terrible. Just thinking about it has my jaw clenching and my chest feeling hollow. I get wanting to get away from everything, so I said she was welcome to stay with me and help me renovate the house. Lord knows I could use the help.

With a sigh, I run my hand through my hair. To be honest, I didn't expect her to take me up on it, but she did and here we are.

Charlotte was always a bit of a mystery. Book nerd is the first thing that comes to mind when I think of her. With her blonde hair and blue eyes, she's pretty but reserved. While I may have practically lived at their house, I still didn't see too much of her as she locked herself away in her room with her books rather than going out with friends like the other girls her age. She was quiet and Alex has always been protective of her. When she got her first serious boyfriend, Alex drove us over to his house so he could give him the big brother talk.

The ringing of my cell pulls me out of my thoughts, straightening up and pulling it from my pocket I see Alex's name flash up and grin at the cheesy picture of him that accompanies it.

"Hey, bud, you ok?" I ask, watching a golden retriever running down the beach avoiding the tide. His owner follows shortly after, trying to get him back on his leash.

"Yeah, all good, thanks. Just letting you know that Charlotte's flight is scheduled to arrive on time." I chuckle to myself, he's in protective big brother mode already. Some things never change.

"Yeah, I've been checking her flight schedule online. I'll be leaving shortly to pick her up," I reassure him, picking up my coffee mug again. "Stop panicking. I'm going to be the best big brother she's ever had."

"Jerk," he says with a rough laugh and I swear I hear his eyes roll. "Thanks again for this, man. She really needs the distance to put herself back together." I hear his sigh over the phone and wonder what the hell her ex did to her to make Alex so concerned about his sister. This is another level, even for him.

"Hey, don't mention it. I get it. You know how Becky screwed me over." Even her name makes me cringe and sends ice through my veins.

How was I so blind to what was going on?

"Yeah. I knew you'd understand. Thanks, mate. Just... look after her, yeah? She's been through a lot."

"Of course. You know I will. I better get going. Catch you later, man."

"Cool, thanks, man."

Hanging up, I down the rest of my coffee and head inside to get my truck keys.

CHAPTER THREE

Charlotte

Things moved quickly after I accepted Ollie's offer. Mum sorted out my ticket and visa as promised, and I handed in my notice at work. Now here I am, gripping the armrest of my plane seat like my life depends on it. And who knows, it actually might! Planes scare the crap out of me. It blows my mind how a metal box full of people can stay in the air. People who say you're more likely to be in a car crash than a plane crash seem to forget one key fact. If your car crashes, you're still on the ground. If your car crashes, you aren't going to plummet to the earth and die in a fiery inferno. So excuse me if that little bit of information doesn't reassure me in the slightest.

Jolting forward as the wheels hit the tarmac below, I let out a sigh of relief that I'm back on solid ground and release my desperate grip on the armrests. The seatbelt sign goes off, and I unbuckle mine and sit back to watch chaos ensue. It amazes me how people rush to grab their bags from the overhead lockers when we all have to get off the same way, and not until the doors are open.

What's the rush?

Powering on my phone, I send Mum a quick text to let her know I arrived in one piece and swiftly turn it back off. There's no one else I need to check in with, and seeing Mum's reply will just make me more nervous and cause me to start second guessing this decision. Is travelling thousands of miles away from my family really the smartest decision right now? They've been the only thing keeping me going.

Inhaling deeply, I hold it for a moment before releasing it slowly and trying to steady myself. This will be good for me.

Once the door to the plane opens, I watch the mad dash of people to get off. It's not like most of us need to stand and wait at the luggage carousel for ages anyway, right?

Thanking the crew, I step off the plane and stand tall, pulling my shoulders back and deciding that this is the new start I've been craving. The one I deserve.

***

Walking through arrivals, I look around for Ollie. Alex said he'd meet me here and showed me a recent photo of him so I'd know who I was looking for. Not that I'd forget him after all the time he spent at our house over the years. He's changed since he was at university with Alex. He's still sinfully attractive. Tall with dark black hair, but now he has a tattoo on his arm and a five o'clock shadow. He's definitely grown up. He could easily be a cover model on one of the romance novels I love so much.

Lost in my thoughts, I keep walking through the terminal until I hear a smooth southern voice shout, "Charlotte!"

Looking over to my left, I spot him emerging from behind a small group of people. In a white vest with his intricate tattoo on full display, he gives me a wave and a smile. It takes an insane amount of willpower not to stop in my tracks at the sight of him and cause a people pile up. Holy moly, his picture did not do him justice. The man is better than a fantasy.

Smiling back, hoping my cheeks aren't the colour of my luggage, I wheel my bright pink case over to him and he takes it from me.

"Hey, stranger," he says, offering me a takeaway coffee. I gratefully accept the caffeinated gift with a beaming smile.

"Thanks! Whoever said diamonds are a girl's best friend was lying. Coffee is. Hands down."

His deep throaty chuckle warms me more than the mouthful of coffee I take. "How was your flight?"

"It was alright. As good as flying through the air in a death trap can be." Shrugging my shoulders, I run a hand through my unruly hair as I take in the busy terminal around us.

He laughs, shaking his head. "Right. Alex said you weren't too keen on flying. Advised me to be waiting with a coffee offering." He motions to the cup in my hand, and I nod.

"Not my favourite thing to do, no. But I made it in one piece, so happy days." I brush my hair behind my ear and take a sip of the coffee. Milk, no sugar. Just how I like it.

Thank you, big brother.

"Welcome to North Carolina," Ollie says with a picture perfect smile, leading me to the exit. He's tall and athletic, so I have to speed up to keep pace with his long strides. Not that it's such a hardship having to be behind him, the view is a sight for sore eyes.

"Thanks. And thanks so much for letting me stay with you for a while. The change of scenery is very welcome right now."

I'm starting to get excited about this. No one knows me, I can just get on with my life, not worrying about the people gossiping behind me or sending me looks of pity.

"Don't mention it. You're doing me a favour." He offers me a kind smile over his shoulder, the green in his eyes catching the sun and bewitching me. I need to pull myself together. I've just arrived and I'm already drooling over my housemate.

What is wrong with me?

Ollie pays for the parking, even though I offer, and we head to a blue truck, which he unlocks and throws my case in like it weighs nothing. Moving to the passenger's side, I climb in, letting out a sigh of relief that I made it.

As we pull out of the car park, I glance over at the man behind the wheel. Wearing only a white vest over his torso, his impressive biceps are on full display. The ink working its way up one is intricate and detailed and I find my gaze following it up to his shoulders. Realising I'm gawking, I blush and turn to look out of the window. He's doing me a favour, letting me stay with him for a while, and I'm over here ogling him like a hormonal teenager.

"So Alex said you're opening a B&B?" I say, breaking the comfortable silence that has stretched between us as we make the drive back to his house.

"That's the plan. My grandparents left their house to me when they passed. It's sat gathering dust so I thought I could renovate it and rent it out, since moving in isn't an option right now."

"Did you spend a lot of time here growing up?" I ask, genuinely curious.

"Yeah, my parents both worked a lot during the summer break, so they'd fly me over to stay with Gram and Pops. Some of the best memories I have were made with them." A smile stretches across his face as he gets lost in his memories. Pulling a pair of Aviator sunglasses from the dash, he slips them on and focuses on the road ahead. Before he can catch me checking him out again, I turn to look out the window.

Silence stretches between us again and after I catch him looking over at me a couple of times, I decide to bite the bullet and ask the question weighing on my mind. "What did my brother tell you?"

If he's surprised by my sudden question, he doesn't show it. "Not much. Just said that your ex screwed you over big time and you needed to get away. A fresh start."

Nodding, I internally thank my brother for not going into detail when airing my dirty laundry. I don't want Ollie's pity, that's not why I'm here. I want to be Charlotte again. Not the poor woman who was humiliated and had her heart broken so publicly.

"That about sums it up." A self-depreciating laugh slips past my lips and I play with the hem of my t-shirt.

"Men suck, right?" he jokes, looking over at me through the tinted lenses. The sun shines through the truck window, lighting up his face and making me take notice of his defined cheekbones and dark five o'clock shadow.

"You can say that again," I admit, turning away and focusing on the world flying past outside of my window.

"Men suck."

Unable to help myself, I laugh at his lame joke and shake my head in disbelief. He doesn't push any further and I'm grateful for that. I'm sick of talking about it, of thinking about it, of living it. I need a break, and that's exactly what I'm hoping for.

CHAPTER FOUR

Ollie

Once I've given Charlotte a quick tour of the house, I leave her to settle in and find her feet and make my way to the kitchen to make myself a coffee. It's strange how the house feels different with another person here. But maybe it's just because it's her. Rather than my thoughts drifting to recollections of my grandparents and the memories this house is filled with, every spare one is focused on Charlotte.

The ringing of my phone on the counter pulls me from my thoughts. Swiping it from the counter, I answer without checking the ID.

"Hello?"

"Hey, man, how's it going?" my friend Scott's voice asks over the line.

"Hey, man, good, thanks. Just picked Charlotte up from the airport, so letting her settle in."

"She hot?" *Yes.*

"You're married," I deadpan, rolling my eyes at him. He's always been the playboy out of the two of us. That was until he met his match in his wife. She tamed the beast.

"I wasn't asking for me. You know what they say. The best way to get over one woman is to get under another." I can practically hear his grin through the phone and I let out a chuckle.

"Yeah, well that doesn't apply when it's your best mate's sister," I reply, looking through the kitchen window, wanting to move away from where this conversation is heading. As attractive as Charlotte is, she's off limits. End of.

"He won't mind! You're a stand-up guy, he knows that. Hell, I'd let you date my sister."

"You don't have a sister," I point out, shaking my head. He's something else, that's for sure.

"So? If I did, I'd totally let you date her. Just saying."

"You working?" I ask, changing the conversation in case the woman in question decides to walk in at any moment.

"Yeah, heading to Tennessee with a shipment. Thought I'd break up the boredom by calling you."

"You say the nicest things," I joke. "No wonder you convinced Melody to marry you."

"I know, right? Speak of the devil, she's trying to call. I'll talk to you later?"

"Yeah, stay safe, man." Hanging up, I shoot Alex a quick text to let him know we're back at the house and put my phone back on the counter.

With my coffee cup in hand, I head out onto the porch and watch the waves crashing on the beach, the sound so soothing. With the beautiful blue sky, ocean view, and the sun shining down, I can't deny it. This place is something special. Always has been.

A dog barks in the distance and when I look up, I find Charlotte fussing over a Great Dane, chatting with their owner. She's breath taking, and fuck if that isn't unnerving. Gone is the reclusive bookworm from my uni days, and in her place is a gorgeous woman. She's changed into a yellow floral skirt that reaches her knees and a white off the shoulder top that shows a slither of skin at her midriff. My eyes are drawn to the lightly tanned skin on display, wondering if it's as soft as it looks, how it would feel to run my... *abort. Abort!*

Christ, she's been here all of five minutes and I'm already crossing a fucking line. Best friend's sister, the same best friend who's called twice today already to make sure I remembered to pick her up. Who thanked me again and again for helping his little sister out. Who told me what a great mate I am.

I'm so lost in my thoughts, I don't realise she's caught me checking her out until it's too late. She makes her way back to the house and I lean against the railing, sipping on my coffee.

"Hey," she says, sitting in the wicker chair on the porch and glancing back out at the view in wonder. The way her blonde hair frames her face, hiding her soft skin, has me itching to lean over and move it with my fingers. But I restrain myself.

"I can't believe this is your grandparents' place," she says, pulling me from my inner struggle. Her voice is filled with awe and her eyes never leave the view. The house may be a little dilapidated, in need of some work, but it is beautiful and the location is incredible. With a wraparound porch and huge windows, it's impossible to forget you're on the beach with the view of the ocean front and centre.

"Yep. Beautiful, right?" Out of the corner of my eye, I see her eyes leave the beach and find me. She checks me out, trying to be subtle, and it takes effort on my part not to smirk. Instead, I push off the railing and sit in the chair across from hers.

"It's stunning. Why are you renting it out? Why not live here and find another way to make a living? I don't think I could bear to part with it if it were mine," she admits, taking it all in again. The beach, the house, the peacefulness. It's heaven on earth.

"To be honest, I don't know if I could live here without them. It may sound stupid, but all the memories I made in this place were with them. It would feel so empty without them." I miss them terribly as it is. I can't imagine living in the house without them. Not seeing Pops doing a jigsaw on the porch, or Gram baking up a storm in the kitchen. My chest feels hollow just thinking about it.

Her hand reaches across the table and settles on top of

mine, startling me. The electricity her touch causes to race across my skin throws me off kilter. My gaze meets hers and I see the sympathy in them, but more than that. There's something else, does she feel it too?

She squeezes my hand once more and then pulls it back, looking away.

"I get that." She plays with the necklace she's wearing, turning the pendant over in her hand, the motion drawing my gaze as I finish my last mouthful of coffee. "I can't imagine living in my parent's house if they weren't around anymore. It wouldn't feel like home anymore."

"Coffee?" I ask, nodding to the house and watching the smile spread across her face. Her smile does something to me. It's sweet yet sinful, demure yet enticing. My heart rate picks up, as if it's being called with a siren song.

"I thought you'd never ask," she teases, following me inside.

Leading her into the kitchen, I make us both a coffee. Putting the kettle on to boil, I grab her an old china mug from one of the dilapidated cupboards, setting it down next to mine, and add some instant coffee to each.

"It'll be popular with tourists, it's beautiful." The sincerity in her voice makes me smile. She gets this place. Grabbing the milk from the refrigerator, I add a splash to both mugs and return it.

"It's dated. It needs a lot of work, but I'm up for the challenge," I say, handing her a mug of coffee and leaning against the island in the kitchen. I definitely saw the house through rose-coloured glasses when I was a kid. Or maybe it just got worn down over the years that have passed. Either way, I can't rent out rooms in its current state.

"Thanks. So what is your plan?" she asks as she takes a sip. I don't miss the slight grimace at the taste of her coffee and try to hold back my smile. Not an instant fan it seems.

"I want to redecorate. Turn the entryway into a reception. Add an en suite to the fifth bedroom and put a door in between the bathroom and the third bedroom. That way all rooms will be en suite. No one wants to go to a B&B and share a bathroom with strangers. It depends on how money goes. I may have to open up first using just the three bedrooms and close for further refurbishment when profits are in."

"That makes sense. It's a stunning location. I'm sure it won't be hard to get business." Her eyes drift to the view from the kitchen window. The beach is amazing. Having it right on your doorstep is a blessing. Nothing beats a morning run on the beach or having your morning coffee while watching the sunrise.

"I hope so. I love it here." Looking out the window at the view, I smile into my mug.

"I can see why you made some wonderful memories here growing up."

Smiling as I reminisce, I say, "Yeah. Gram loved to bake. I'd go out with Pops and when we came back, the house would smell like a bakery."

"I wish I could bake. I'm awful in the kitchen. Alex jokes that I'm the only person he knows who can burn pasta." She rolls her eyes at that and I chuckle. She's nothing like I remember, little Charlotte is all grown up. Her long blonde hair frames her pale face, the only splash of colour coming from her pink lipstick. She looks exhausted, beautiful, but exhausted. Alex said she'd been struggling with the aftermath of her breakup, but I didn't realise just how much. A part of me wants to reach out and pull her to me, hold her close and protect her from the world. The other part wants to show her how a real man would appreciate her. Every inch.

"I can teach you to make something, if you like. Gram made sure I spent plenty of time learning all the basics." The smile that graces her face makes me proud that I put it there. I vow to myself that while she's here, I'll do everything in my power to keep it there.

"We're trying to do the place up, not burn it down." She grins at me, and I enjoy watching her relax around me. It makes her seem younger, less jaded by the world. Her blue eyes are so pale, they're striking. Combined with her golden hair and plump lips, she's a knockout and she has no idea.

Laughing, I shake my head and take another sip of my coffee. She's a breath of fresh air, that's for sure.

"So how can I help?" she asks, cocking her head to the side and clasping her mug of coffee to her chest.

"How are you at painting?" I ask, smiling.

"I guess we'll soon find out." She laughs and I see a glimpse of carefree Charlotte. Her eyes light up and she shakes her head.

"Alex said you're an interior design buff?" When I mentioned my plan to her brother, he was quick to say how she had a great eye for design and loved renovating.

"I love redecorating. Furnishing empty spaces. I watch more home improvement shows than you can imagine. Not sure 'buff' is the word I'd use, but I would love to help." The enthusiasm in her voice is impossible to miss.

"Then let's come up with a plan and head to The Home Depot."

CHAPTER FIVE

Charlotte

Walking down the aisles of The Home Depot, Ollie following behind with a trolley, I let my inner designer come out to play. We decided on an ocean theme. Lots of blues and whites. Making it light and airy. I'm far too excited for this renovation project. For the first time in what feels like forever, I'm looking forward to something. Not looking back at everything and overthinking. And it feels great.

Moving down the paint aisle, I scan the tins to find the

perfect colours to complement one another.

"How about this one?" I ask, pointing to a tin of baby blue paint.

"Sure, looks good," Ollie says with a shrug as he grabs a few tins and loads them into the trolley. I turn to look at the darker shades, thinking about which colour will look good with the lighter shade and trying not to notice how his muscles bunch when he lifts the tins.

"Ooo! This one will work nicely. What do you think?" I ask, pointing at the tin labelled Olympic blue.

"Yeah. That'll work." He once again grabs a few tins and adds them to the trolley.

"You're very easy to please," I joke, moving to the white paint section and helping him grab a few tins.

"It's just paint." He chuckles as he steers the trolley round to the paintbrush aisle.

"Rude. This is more than just paint. This is the tools of *artists*," I say with a dramatic flair, shooting him a playful smile.

Laughing, he says, "My apologies, Picasso. Please continue in your quest for the perfect tools for your craft."

"Thank you." I offer him a dramatic bow and continue on my quest to find the perfect paintbrush, enjoying the sound of his rough chuckle behind me. This house is going to be picture perfect by the time I'm done with it.

As we make our way to the tills to pay, we find ourselves walking through the kitchen aisle. Seeing the new kitchen displays has a lump forming in my throat. Carl and I had a new kitchen fitted earlier this year. Ours was dated and desperately needed updating, but he was reluctant. He said it was an expense we didn't need so I offered to put it all on my credit card and he agreed, assuring me he'd help me pay it back in instalments. Looking back, it made sense that he had no intention of sticking around. Why pay for a kitchen in a house you weren't intending on staying in?

"Hey, where'd you go?" Ollie's soft voice pulls me out of the memory and I startle when his hand rests on the small of my back, the touch heating my skin.

"Sorry, I was miles away," I joke, trying to block out the past and focus on the here and now.

"Yeah, I saw. Wanna talk about it?" he asks, his kind eyes boring into mine as we join the queue to pay for our materials. His forehead is pulled down into a frown, and I find myself wanting to reach out and smooth it away. Wanting to reach out and touch him.

"No, I'm good. Thanks." I offer him a tight smile and am thankful when he drops it. This is a fresh start, memories like that have no place here. I want to leave all my baggage behind and be my old self again. And the last thing I need is to throw myself into something new with my brother's best friend.

CHAPTER SIX

Ollie

After a productive day moving the furniture out of the living room and foyer and repainting the rooms, we decide to order a pizza and call it a day. The place is already looking more modern. Gone is the dated wallpaper Gram put up all those years ago, and in its place is a light, open space. Credit where it's due, Charlotte has a good eye for this stuff. I was worried I'd be sad to see the place change so much, with it being my last piece of my grandparents. But no one can take the memories of them from me, and they're the most valuable thing I can have. A house without them isn't a home.

"Pepperoni ok?" I ask, as I bring up the local pizza delivery website on my phone to place our order.

"Sounds good," she calls over her shoulder. She's currently boxing up utensils and pans from the kitchen so we can make a start on painting it tomorrow. Bent over by the counter, I try not to let my eyes linger on her arse clad in denim, but I am a man. How she fills them out should be a crime. I have to avert my gaze and remind myself that she's my best friend's sister once again. It doesn't get much more off limits than that.

"Sorted. Thirty minutes and it's all ours," I say, walking to the fridge to grab a cold beer. "Beer?"

"Not for me, thanks. Just a water, if you don't mind?" She tapes up the box she just filled and places it in the corner with the others.

Grabbing a glass from one of the cupboards she's yet to empty, I make her a cold glass of water and pass it over to where she's standing.

"Thanks." She smiles before taking a sip, leaning against the counter and looking around the bare room.

"We made better progress than I thought we would today," I admit, taking a swig of my beer and enjoying the taste.

"Yeah, it's looking brighter already. I'm thinking kitchen and dining room tomorrow. Then we can tackle the upstairs at the weekend." Her forehead crinkles as she thinks up her plan and I stifle the smile I can feel growing. She's cute.

"Sounds like a plan. Then once all the painting is done,

we can think about furniture and ornaments and all that stuff." I motion my hands around to the bare interior before taking another slug of beer.

"All that stuff." She laughs, shaking her head. The sound makes me smile, and I find myself wanting to make her laugh more often. "Spoken like a true designer."

Chuckling, I say, "Never claimed to be. You're the buff, remember?"

The conversation is easy and before I know it, the doorbell rings and the pizza is here. Charlotte grabs a couple of plates and we sit on the floor of the newly decorated living room. Since most of the furniture has been moved into the dining room while we were painting, we have to make do with conversation over dinner rather than TV.

"So, what's your story?" she asks, sitting back on her heels and looking over at me. Her bright blue eyes seem to look straight through to my soul. It's both unnerving and refreshing.

"Wow, cut right to the chase why don't you?" I joke, grabbing a slice of pizza and taking a bite.

"Sorry, I didn't mean to pry. I'm just curious as to why you're renovating the house now. You said you needed the money. Did something happen?" Her question is hesitant, like she knows it is a sensitive subject and she knows what it feels like to not want to talk about something.

Sighing, I finish my slice of pizza and take a long drink of my beer to ease the tightness forming in my throat.

"Yeah. My ex happened," I croak, shaking my head at the memories of that back-stabbing witch.

"Shitty ex? Been there." She laughs, but it's half-hearted

and doesn't reach her eyes. Her gaze finds her hands and she links her fingers. I find myself wanting to fly halfway across the world to punch this douche in the face.

"Turns out she was only after my money. Ran up credit card bills in my name and when the money dried up, so did her interest in me. I'm still beating myself up over the fact that I didn't see what was happening." I take another swig of my beer, trying to replace the bitter taste talking about Becky leaves in my mouth.

"Wow. What a bitch," Charlotte says, shaking her head, the disgust evident in her tone. Her brows pinch together as she scowls at the thought.

I give a humourless laugh and rub a hand over my face, the tightness in my chest easing at her flippant comment. "Yeah, apparently so. When she realised I didn't have any more money for her to spend, she found someone new and moved on."

"Good riddance to bad rubbish," she says, lifting her water glass for me to toast.

"Ain't that the truth," I admit, clinking my bottle to her glass and then taking a drink. It surprises me how easy it is to talk to Charlotte. It's not forced, not uncomfortable, and neither of us feel the need to fill any of the silences.

"I'm surprised her beady eyes didn't light up at this place. I'm sure you'd earn a pretty penny from selling it." I watch her gaze flit around the room, smiling at her fast-formed love for the house.

"I never told her about it. Looking back now, that probably should have been my first clue that the relationship wasn't working. The fact that I didn't want her to know about this place. I wasn't looking to sell, and I guess subconsciously, I knew she'd push for it." Hindsight is a wonderful thing. I kick myself now for not seeing what sort of person she was. But love truly does make you blind. I thought we were meant to be. I made excuses for her crappy behaviour. And look where that left me. Broke and broken.

"So she never met your grandparents?" Charlotte asks, grabbing another slice of pizza and looking up at me in curiosity. The genuine interest in her eyes has me opening up more to her than I have to anyone in a long time.

"No. We were only together for eighteen months and they passed before then." My voice breaks slightly, the thought that they've gone still hurts even though it's been a few years now.

"I'm sorry." I offer her a smile in thanks and help myself to the penultimate slice from the box.

"What about you, what's your story?" I ask, taking a bite out of my greasy goodness and eyeing her curiously. Other than what I remember from years ago, and what little her brother has told me, I know very little about this beautiful woman.

I see the shutters come down immediately. Her entire body tenses and she pales. Whatever she's running from, it's hurting her. And she's not ready to talk about it.

"I, uh…" She avoids eye contact and I feel like a dick for bringing it up and making her uncomfortable. *Way to ruin a good night, hotshot.*

"Hey, don't worry about it. We don't have to talk about it. Let's talk through our plan for tomorrow," I offer, trying to bring back the laid back atmosphere we'd created during dinner. She offers me a grateful smile and launches into her ideas for the kitchen.

Whoever her ex was, he sure did one hell of a number on her.

CHAPTER SEVEN

Charlotte

After the best night's sleep I can remember having in a long time, I roll over and grab my phone. Turning it on, I see a message from my brother and smile.

Alex: How's your holiday going?

Me: Good. This place is gorgeous! The beach is literally at your front door and I'm in decorating heaven.

Alex: You're so lame.

Me: Shut up.

Alex: You doing ok? Ollie looking after
you?

Rolling my eyes, I dial his number and he answers straight away.

"Hey, Lottie," he says, slightly out of breath and I know I've caught him on his way out of the gym. *Who goes to the gym on their lunch break? Weirdo.*

"You know I'm an adult, right? I can look after myself."

"I know. But it doesn't mean other people can't look out for you too," he reasons and I shake my head at him. He's always been like this. Mr. Protective. It's sweet but since Carl, it's gotten worse.

"How're Mum and Dad?" I ask, sitting up and stretching, wondering if Ollie is up yet.

"Enjoying having their space back, I assume," he teases and I laugh.

"I'm a great housemate, thank you very much!" Walking over to my suitcase, which I haven't bothered unpacking yet, I start to pull together an outfit for today.

"Sure you are. But you're cramping their style." I freeze.

"Never. Ever. Say that again. Gross." I shudder at the thought and throw my chosen outfit onto the bed, checking my reflection in the dresser mirror.

Alex's bark of laughter has me pulling my phone away from my ear.

"You're too easy to rile. You're good though, right?"

"I am. I really am. Stop worrying. I need a caffeine fix so I'm going to go, but I'll call you soon, ok?"

"Ok. Love you, Lot."

"Love you too."

Once I've dressed and brushed my teeth, I make my way downstairs and find Ollie in the kitchen rummaging around in the fridge. With a pair of fitted pale blue jeans, my eyes are drawn to his pert bum. He definitely has grown up. But I need to stop perving over my housemate and focus on the job at hand. My heart was just broken in spectacular fashion, the last thing I need is another man messing with my head.

"Morning!" I say, a lot chirpier than intended and internally chastising myself.

Ollie turns to greet me, flashing me a smile. He's wearing a short-sleeved checked shirt that makes me think of a cowboy. I bet he'd look good in a cowboy hat. Straddling…

He pulls me from my ridiculous thoughts, my face no doubt flushed, when he speaks. "Morning. Sleep well?"

"Like a baby, thanks. And the view from that bedroom is to die for! This B&B is going to be fully booked all the time." I would gladly book a room for the year. The beach, the weather, the house. This place is amazing.

"That's the plan." He chuckles, putting the milk carton on the counter and shutting the fridge door. "Coffee?"

"God, yes, please." Collapsing onto a stool in front of the island, I run a hand through my messy hair and take in the kitchen. I saw it last night, but now it's revamp day, I pay more attention to the details. It's a pale-yellow colour, dated but homey. The work surfaces are white granite and look good as new. The appliances all seem in relatively good condition too, which is good news, especially since Ollie mentioned the budget wasn't great.

The sound of a boiling kettle draws my attention. Looking back to Ollie, I see him adding instant coffee to a mug and waiting on the kettle to boil.

"Seriously? I thought Americans were all about real coffee. Not instant crap. Have you not learnt anything while living over here?" I joke. I had thought it yesterday but didn't want to make a bad second 'first' impression by mentioning it.

Ollie chuckles, a deep sound that comes from his chest and makes me smile. Running a hand through his messy hair, my eyes follow the tensing of his muscles at the movement. His ink draws my attention once again, the black and white hourglass on his forearm intriguing me. I've never found tattoos overly sexy on a guy before, but on him, I'm mesmerized. I want to trace every inch of them.

"I didn't realise you were a coffee snob. What's wrong with instant coffee?" he asks, turning to face me and leaning up against the kitchen counter with his arms folded over his chest. It takes every ounce of my self-control to keep my gaze on his and not let it drift down to his bulging biceps.

"What's right with it? How don't you have a coffee machine? That needs adding to our list. A good B&B would definitely serve decent coffee." I would walk out of a B&B if they didn't serve decent coffee. It's surely an arrestable offence.

"You reckon?" He chuckles at me, clearly thinking I am ridiculous.

"Ummm… yeah! B&B. It stands for bed and breakfast so you know those two things need to be on point. And coffee is a staple of a good breakfast," I say, watching as he turns to add the water to my sorry excuse for a coffee and shakes his head with a smile.

"Milk? Or does that offend you too?" he jokes, looking over his shoulder at me and I roll my eyes.

"Yes to milk, thank you." Once he's made it, I take it from his outstretched hand, trying to ignore how my traitorous heart skips a beat when our fingers touch. Taking a sip, I hold back a grimace. Definitely not great coffee, but hey… first thing in the morning, I'll take whatever caffeine fix I can get.

"So other than a coffee machine, I'm thinking we need to replace the blinds, they're super dated. And then we'll need a new table and chairs, this one has seen better days." He nods to the furniture in question.

Looking over at the small kitchen table and four chairs, I frown. They look fine, a bit worn, but nothing a lick of paint won't fix.

"Why don't we sand them down and paint them a pale blue? It'll match the blue we're using on the walls and save some money," I offer, taking another sip of my coffee.

"Yeah, you think that'll work?" he asks, leaning on the island and looking over at me.

"Yeah, there's nothing wrong with them. They just need a bit of TLC." I have watched more DIY programmes than I care to admit. It's a relatively easy fix to spruce them up, and a lot more cost efficient.

"Ok, so more paint, some sandpaper, a coffee machine apparently." He quirks his brow at me in amusement and I bite my lip to hold in my smile. "Blinds, new tableware, and that should do for now?"

"Sounds good." I take another drink from my mug and must pull a face as I swallow because he chuckles and shakes his head.

"Tell you what, your royal highness. Why don't we grab a coffee and some breakfast on our way to The Home Depot?" he asks, turning and grabbing his truck keys from the side.

"Now you're talking." I smile and walk around the island to pour the remainder of the liquid atrocity down the sink. I reach for my bag from the table and follow him to the door.

CHAPTER EIGHT

Ollie

H olding the door for Charlotte, I motion for her to enter first and follow her in. Walking up to the counter, I take a minute to browse the new additions to the wall mounted menu before picking what I'll order. I may not mind the instant stuff, but I can appreciate good coffee. Turning to Charlotte, I notice how uncomfortable she looks. She's playing with the hem of her royal blue t-shirt and her eyes are darting around the shop. It's a side I've not seen before, and I don't like it.

"Are you ok?" I ask, concerned she may not be feeling too good. She hasn't eaten since last night, maybe she's feeling light-headed.

"Yeah. I'm... not too great with crowds," she admits quietly, looking like she'd rather be anywhere than here. This place is pretty popular, being so close to the beach, so it's already filling up. A group of teenagers are laughing and taking selfies by the door, as an older couple sit nearby reading the morning paper.

"Want to grab it to take away?" I offer, pointing back in the direction of the door we came through a moment ago.

"Do you mind?" She looks so embarrassed, I hate it. Her shoulders have slumped and her eyes are focused on the floor. I want to pull her into my arms and offer to fight her demons.

"Of course not. I'd rather be outside in this weather anyway. I can show you around the area." Offering her a reassuring smile when her gaze finds mine, I turn to the barista and give her my order, before looking back at Charlotte.

"Oh, can I have a large coconut latte with a salted caramel shot please?" she asks, and I smile at the drink choice. It's very her.

"And two bagels to go as well please," I say, handing over my credit card and refusing Charlotte's outstretched hand of cash.

She smiles but it doesn't reach her eyes, she's really not comfortable here. I wonder why that is. Maybe coffee shops remind her of her ex?

It took most of the morning to cover all the surfaces and masking tape all the skirting, but by early afternoon we are well on the way to having a new kitchen. The pale blue Charlotte picked is perfect. It makes the room look brighter while also fitting in with the nautical theme she suggested. She says she's no interior designer, but I beg to differ. The woman knows what she's doing.

Hearing a knock at the door, I put my paint roller down and move towards the front entrance, leaving Charlotte to it as she bops along to the playlist blaring out from her phone.

Opening the door, I grin when I find my friend Scott staring back at me. At six foot five, with shaggy brown hair and matching beard, he never changes. We worked together for a few years and developed a great friendship. I was best man at his wedding to his wife, Melody, last year. When he *finally* managed to put a ring on it.

"Hey, bud, what're you doing here?" I ask him, pleasantly surprised by his shock appearance. I pull him in for a hug and slap him on the back.

"I was nearby for work and thought I'd drop by and say hey. This place is looking great," he says, taking in the newly decorated foyer as I motion for him to come inside.

"Thanks, we're making good progress." It's coming along much better than I expected. Charlotte really does have a good eye.

"We?" he asks, quirking a brow, and I remember my manners.

"Oh, yeah." I lead him into the kitchen where Charlotte

is putting down her paintbrush and introduce them. "Scott, this is Charlotte, Charlotte, this is Scott."

"Oh! So you're the best friend's sister. Pleasure to meet you," Scott says, shaking her hand in his huge one and offering her one of his friendly smiles. "How're you liking it here?"

"It's lovely. Puts back home to shame." Charlotte smiles back and looks over at me. The light catching her blue eyes and making them shine, stealing my breath. For a moment time stands still and it's just the two of us. When she turns back to Scott the moment is broken, leaving me wondering if it's all in my head. "Would you like a coffee?"

Scott looks at the new coffee machine that Charlotte is getting ready and raises a brow at me.

"I'd love one, thanks. Going up in the world, are we?" he jokes, looking at me with a teasing smirk. He knows I'm the most low-maintenance guy you could find.

"Someone is a coffee snob and turned her nose up at instant coffee so I had to branch out," I say, rolling my eyes at the look he gives me.

"I'm not a snob. I merely pointed out that your coffee tasted like dirt and if you were going to be offering people breakfast, then you had to offer them decent coffee too," Charlotte reasons, grabbing three mugs from the cupboard above her head. I like seeing her move about the kitchen like she's comfortable here.

Where did that thought come from?

"Woman's got a point," Scott says, grinning at me. Bastard is enjoying this.

"Don't you start." I groan, pulling out a chair and

planting myself in it while Charlotte plays hostess. I'm pleased she is starting to feel more at home here. I want her to relax and be herself.

"So Scott, what do you do?" Charlotte asks, as she passes him a freshly made cup of fancy coffee.

"I'm a hauler," he replies, taking a swig of his coffee and pulling out a seat.

"A what now?" Her eyebrows scrunch in confusion and it's adorable.

Laughing, I answer for Scott, "Fancy name for a truck driver."

"Oh, I see." She sits beside me, taking a sip of her coffee and looks between us. "Is that how you two met?"

"Yeah, we used to work together. The company had a bit of a wobble last year, so they offered voluntary surplus out to any drivers happy to take it. I knew I wanted time to sort this place out, so I took it and here I am." I look over at Scott and he's nodding, leaning back in his chair and resting his mug on his knee.

"Voluntary surplus? Is that like redundancy? They pay you a settlement figure and you leave?" Tracing the rim of her mug, she tilts her head and looks up at me.

"Yep, that's the one. Was a decent amount, gave me a little bit of a buffer and some money to pay off the bills I was left with, and a little left over to use to turn this place around. I don't miss the long days, that's for sure."

"Yeah, you may have had the right idea. These hours are killing me. And Melody is always on at me for not being home enough." Sighing, he shakes his head. I get where his wife is coming from. Sometimes you're gone for almost a week doing one shipment. It's full on. It must be tough for her. Becky, my ex, never seemed to mind. But now I know that's because I was off earning and she could live her best life off of my credit card. Shaking those thoughts away, I look at my friend. He definitely looks tired. It is a rough job, but it pays well.

"I need to see you guys. I don't think I've seen Melody since the wedding," I admit regretfully. The only problem with being so far away is that it isn't as easy to visit my friends.

"You do. Melody has said as much." His face lights up as he has an idea. "Hey, I'm back in this neck of the woods next week. Why don't I see if Melody fancies tagging along and we can drop by?"

"That would be awesome. We can go for dinner." After the breakup, I'm not too proud to admit that I didn't cope the best. I distanced myself from my friends. Trust became a big thing for me. But Scott and Melody never gave up on me. They're the closest thing to family I have over here now, and I'm forever grateful for them.

"Cool, I'll run it past the wife and see what she thinks. So, Charlotte, how's living with this bum?" He nods his head to me with a laugh and she joins in.

Chuckling, I lean back and watch the two of them swap stories. I've missed this. Shutting myself off from anyone who could hurt me again may have felt necessary, but I was the only one missing out.

CHAPTER NINE

Charlotte

With the soft yellow glow of the sun shining down on the sand, I have to squint to look up to see Ollie coming down the porch steps. Carrying the tired looking dining table, his grey vest gives me a mouth-watering view of his strong arms. The ink wrapped around one does nothing to hide the muscles bunching beneath under the weight of the furniture.

As he sets it down in front of me, on top of the old bedsheet we've laid down to stop sand from getting to it, I grab the sandpaper we picked up from the hardware store and get to work.

"So what are we doing?" he asks, wiping the bead of sweat from his forehead and causing a flush to heat my cheeks as I imagine what sweat would look like dripping from his bare chest.

Clearing my throat, I say, "Sanding down the table, then we can start painting it and it will look good as new."

"That simple, huh?" He laughs and I smile at the sound, peering up at him. The sunlight is basking him in a warm glow that makes him seem almost angelic. Ironic, considering my thoughts at the view are anything but.

"That simple," I agree, nodding to the sandpaper by the table leg.

Pulling his phone from his pocket, he flicks through it for a moment before the soft sound of Kane Brown fills the air.

"You're a Kane fan?" I ask, surprised that we have that in common.

"Yeah. Last time your brother was visiting, he had it on repeat all the time. Kinda grows on you." His cheeky grin has butterflies fluttering in my stomach. My head is telling me to be smart, to put some distance between us and not jump into something new when I'm still so fragile. Not to mention the fact that he's my brother's best friend. But my heart… my heart is saying this man is something special. And the tug of war between the two is beginning to make me dizzy.

"Alex got me into his music too. His voice is so soothing," I say, pulling myself from the flurry of thoughts flying around in my head. Music has always been an escape of mine. Carl hated my music choices, so after we broke up, I listened to my playlists on repeat. A rebellion of sorts I guess you could say.

"Yeah, your brother has good taste. But don't tell him I said that, it'll go to his head." We both laugh at that. The easy conversation and shared memories have me letting myself relax and just enjoying the moment. It's refreshing.

Working in sync, we let the music fill the comfortable silence between us. Humming along to the songs I love, standing in paradise, I can't help but feel at peace. The world around me is still, other than the soothing sound of the waves crashing on the shore, there's nothing. This is what I need.

We're applying the first coat of paint to the table when I feel something wet hit the hand I have resting on the table top. Looking down, I see the splotch of blue paint on my skin. My eyes meet Ollie's, and his cheeky smirk tells me it was anything but an accident.

"Seriously? How old are you?" I laugh, shaking my head and grabbing a rag from the floor to wipe my hand.

"What's up, sweetheart? Scared to get a little dirty?" His tone is teasing but my insides heat at the word *dirty* slipping from his lips. God, if this man doesn't spark all kinds of feelings in me.

Dipping my brush in the paint, I quickly stand on my tiptoes and wipe it across his nose, laughing at how he now resembles a Smurf. His eyes widen in surprise before a devious grin makes its way to his face. Sensing I may have bitten off more than I can chew, I take a tentative step backwards.

"Game on," he says as he forgoes a brush and dips his finger into the paint. Spinning on my heels, I make a run for it, laughing like a lunatic.

He tugs on my shirt, pulling me back against his chest and before I can right myself, he wipes his finger along my cheek, coating it in blue paint. Turning in his arm, I stare up at him, the remnants of blue paint still covering his nose, and I laugh.

His smile is blinding, putting the scenery to shame as it dazzles me in the warm glow of the sun. The soft feel of his thumb running across my cheek has my heartbeat speeding up. Staring into his emerald eyes, I'm hypnotised. Everything else ceases to exist. In this moment, it's just the two of us. Unconsciously, I find myself leaning into his touch, soaking up the warmth of his skin. Time stands still as he leans toward me, his gaze locked on my lips.

Just as he's about to kiss me, something knocks into me, causing me to pull back in surprise.

"Lexie!" A flustered woman appears by my side, grabbing her energetic dog and attaching the leash she's carrying to the dog's collar.

"I'm so sorry. She is easily excited by people, she didn't mean any harm," she reassures us while trying to calm down the golden retriever. Her tail is wagging so ferociously, I'm surprised she hasn't taken off.

"It's no problem." I laugh, stroking Lexie's shiny coat and trying to process what the hell just happened.

What are we doing?

Stealing a glance at Ollie, I notice he's already gone

back to painting the table, our moment broken. Lexie soaks up the attention she's getting from me, attention that for a split second, I thought Ollie wanted. But now I'm left wondering if it was a mistake.

CHAPTER TEN

Ollie

Affter our almost kiss on the beach this afternoon, I tried to pull back. While I can't deny the connection between Charlotte and I, she's Alex's little sister. I can't betray his trust like that. I mean, it's probably nothing. We're both hurting and looking for some comfort, right?

Scott called yesterday to say he was heading this way on business again, like he said. Melody agreed to tag along, excited at the thought of meeting for dinner at a nearby diner. Although she'd probably more excited at the thought of playing matchmaker, knowing her. Charlotte seemed nervous at the thought, but insisted she wanted to meet them.

"Melody is great. I promise you'll get on like a house on fire," I tell her as I navigate my truck through traffic toward the diner. Her fingers are playing with the material of her skirt, a quirk I recognise as her trying to calm her nerves.

"I'm sure I will," she says, smiling over at me, but it doesn't quite reach her eyes. I don't know why it bothers me so much, but I hate the idea of her being uncomfortable.

"If you want to leave early, just let me know. It's no trouble," I'm quick to reassure her as I pull into the parking lot, finding a space and turning the engine off.

"I'll be fine, honestly." With a slightly brighter smile, she opens the door and jumps out, with me following her lead. Her red skirt swings in the breeze and my gaze follows the movement, stopping at her black heels. As much as I tell myself not to, I can't help imagine what she'd look like in just those heels. As many times as I remind myself to back the fuck up, to remember that she's Alex's little sister, I'm still bewitched by her. I crave her like a drug, needing a fix more than my next breath.

As we enter the diner, I spot the couple immediately and grin. Placing my hand on Charlotte's back, I lead her toward the table. Melody hasn't changed. Her brown hair is tied in a bun on the top of her head, and her red lips curve into a smile when she spots us.

"Well, look who it is." Melody laughs. "I thought you'd vanished into thin air."

"I know, I've been a shit friend. I'm sorry." She stands

and pulls me into a hug as Scott does the same to Charlotte.

"You're forgiven." Turning to Charlotte, she grins as she says, "And you must be Charlotte. Scott's told me about how you're classing up this bum." She bumps her hip into mine, and I shake my head in exasperation.

"Hey, be nice. Charlotte, this is Melody. She's Scott's caregiver."

Scott guffaws at my comment and pulls Melody back into the booth they were occupying. Motioning for Charlotte to sit opposite, I slide in after her.

"It's nice to meet you," she offers, folding her hands in her lap as she takes in the place. It's not some fancy restaurant, but it's one of our favourite places. I used to come here with my grandparents during the summers. With its bright red booths and white tables, it reminds me of a set from *Grease*. The jukebox in the corner is always in use and while this place is never packed, I've never seen it empty either.

"You too. So how did you end up in our little town? Scott said your brother is a friend of Ollie's?" Melody definitely hasn't changed. She's still as nosey as the first night Scott and I met her in that club where she worked behind the bar.

"I was looking for a change of scenery, and Ollie was looking for cheap labour," she jokes, and I bump my shoulder with hers in protest.

"Cheap? Miss 'You need a top of the range coffee machine, no one drinks instant'." She rolls her eyes in exasperation, and I have to bite back my laugh. She's adorable.

"Girl has a point," Melody pipes up, politely flagging

down the waitress so we can order some drinks.

"Thank you!" Charlotte says in triumph, sticking her tongue out at me like a child and making me chuckle.

By the time our food arrives, conversation is flowing easily and Melody and Charlotte are getting along great. Sure their common interest is mocking me, but if it takes the slump out of her shoulders, she can make fun of me all she likes.

It may have been their wedding, the last time that I saw them together, but they're clearly every bit as in love as then. Scott's hand seems to be permanently attached to her thigh, and she wastes no opportunity to press a kiss to his lips.

When Charlotte asks how they met, Melody tells her their little love story. How they were destined to be together. I've heard it more times than I can count, but even I have to admit that it was fate. They're the definition of soulmates.

As Scott and I pay the bill, I'm sad to see the night end. I've missed these guys more than I realised.

"There's a fair on tonight, we could check it out?" I suggest, reluctant for the night to end, and remembering driving past it on the way here. Scott shakes his head apologetically.

"We'd love to, man. But it's been a long ass day. I think we're just going to crash."

We say goodbye in the parking lot and promise not to leave it so long next time. Charlotte hugs Melody and they exchange numbers, with Melody promising to dish all the dirt on me to her new partner in crime.

***

The fair is in full swing by the time we arrive. There are people everywhere, laughing and having a good time. The colourful lights, electric atmosphere, and cacophony of noise from the crowd is captivating. Leading Charlotte straight to the mobile coffee truck, I order us a coffee each.

She gratefully accepts her drink and I lead her through the crowd, keeping my hand on her back. It feels natural, being with her. Like everything is where it should be.

"This is quite something," she says, taking in our surroundings. Stalls line both sides of the walkway, offering refreshments or the chance to win prizes. Kids line up outside of the rides in excitement and coloured lights are everywhere, lighting up the place. The smell of grilling meat and popcorn fills the air.

I laugh. "Yeah, it tends to get a bit rowdy. They love a good excuse to party. My Gram and Pops used to bring me here every year. This is the first time I've been since they passed."

I feel her hand taking mine and giving it a squeeze, and I'm grateful for the action. It's a strange feeling, opening up to someone. I grieved when I lost my grandparents, of course I did. But I never really talked about them with anyone. I didn't feel like I could, scared the grief would overwhelm me, somehow emasculate me. But with Charlotte, it feels good to talk about them. Remember them and all the joy they brought to my life. I don't feel like less of a man for discussing my feelings, I feel stronger. More alive because she's by my side.

A group of teenagers are laughing up ahead, taking silly group selfies and pulling faces. I smile at the carefree attitude they have, but feel Charlotte tense up beside me. Her demeanour changes in a heartbeat and she freezes.

"You ok?" I ask, taking her other hand in mine and turning her to face me. She's turned white as a sheet and looks like she's about to faint. Her breathing is laboured and she looks terrified, it makes my chest ache.

"Charlotte, sweetheart? Talk to me." I take her coffee and put it down with mine, turning all my attention to the woman before me.

"Can't breathe. Panic attack." She manages to pant, I take her face in my hands and bring her focus to me. It was stupid to bring her here. I knew she got anxious around crowds, but I still brought her to the biggest gathering of people in the state.

"You're ok, sweetheart. Deep breaths. It's just you and me, ok? Watching the sunrise on the beach." Stroking her cheek with the pad of my thumb, I mimic the deep breaths she should be taking, ignoring the curious glances passing people throw our way.

Her breathing is still frantic, her hands have moved to grip mine on her face. The terror in her face wrecks me. What happened to shatter this incredible woman in front of me? What did her ex do to her?

"Can... we... go?" she gasps out and I nod, wrapping an arm around her waist and guiding her away from the crowd. She clings to me like I'm her life raft in a tempestuous ocean, and she's being pulled under.

CHAPTER ELEVEN

Charlotte

"**D**o you want to talk about earlier?" Ollie asks, handing me a mug of coffee which I gratefully accept. We're back at the beach house now, sitting on the sofa, and the mortification is setting in.

"It was just a panic attack. I get them sometimes. Sorry you had to witness it," I whisper, mortified that he saw me at my worst. *Good going, Charlotte.*

I thought I was making progress. Letting go of my fears and just enjoying the here and now. But when I saw those kids with their phones, taking pictures they'd no doubt upload to social media, I felt sick. *What if someone recognised me?*

"Don't apologise. Maybe talking about it will help?" His tone isn't pushy, it's friendly and reassuring. Despite my irrational fears, I feel safe here, with him.

Sighing, I take another sip of my coffee. Unsure of where to start. "I'm not a fan of having my photo taken."

"Few people are." He smiles playfully, and I let out a breath I didn't realise I was holding, my shoulders dropping.

"Smartphones make me anxious. Technology is amazing. Being able to keep in touch with friends and family all over the world at just the touch of a button is incredible. I'm not knocking that. But it's also terrifying. It's there forever. No taking it back. Even if you delete it, it could have been screenshot and sent to multiple people by then. One flippant comment made years ago, one awful photo, can find its way back to haunt you. The most humiliating part of your life can be viewed again and again for people's amusement and there is nothing you can do about it. It is brutal and terrifying.

"I panic if I see someone taking a photo where I may be in the shot, worrying it may end up on social media. How pathetic is that? I'm terrified of being seen."

"I get it. You're desperate to fade into the background. Go through life unnoticed. But sweetheart, I notice you. You're all I see." His words make me gasp, causing butterflies to take flight in my stomach. His hand finds mine and the warmth of his touch seeps into my skin, thawing the ice in my veins.

"I'm scared, Ollie. So scared." I admit, looking into his dark green eyes and seeing nothing but compassion. He squeezes my hand, rubbing his thumb over my fingers in a soothing gesture.

"You never have to be afraid with me. You can trust me, Charlotte. I promise."

Staring into his eyes, I can see the sincerity in them shining back at me. I truly believe he would never hurt me, that he would have my back. Not because he's my brother's best friend, but because he's a good man. A great man. And he cares about me.

"I know," I whisper in return.

"Will you ever tell me your story?" Ollie says, as he lets go of my hand and we sit in the living room, sipping our coffee. The silence is stifling. I feel like I'm suffocating in my own head.

"It's embarrassing and makes me feel sick to my stomach just thinking about it." Squeezing my eyes shut at the thought, I take a deep breath and shake my head.

"I want to help." His hand rests on my knee and the warmth from the gesture floods my body once again.

"You have. You have no idea how much you have." And it's true. I've felt more like myself these past few weeks than I have in as long as I can remember.

***

Ollie

I stand to take my now empty mug to the kitchen, thinking I should stop pushing her if she isn't ready, when I hear her whisper.

"My ex cheated on me." Her soft confession surprises me, and I freeze where I am, in case she continues.

She doesn't.

"That says more about him than you, sweetheart." *What an idiot. Who would cheat on the perfect woman?*

"I only found out when he proposed to the other woman live on social media."

Well, *fuck me*. That I was not expecting.

"What?" I turn to face her and wait for her to continue. She's leaning forward, her arms wrapped around her knees, as if she's trying to protect herself from the painful memories. It physically pains me to see her like this. I'd do anything to take it away.

"I'm surprised you didn't see the video. It was liked and shared so many times, became quite the hit. I was tagged in it constantly. People I didn't know started commenting on my relationship. Either pitying me or mocking me. To be honest, I'm not sure which is worse."

Walking back over to the couch, I sit and take her hand in mine. She sends me a grateful smile. I figured something bad had gone down with her ex, but this? I never expected this.

"My heart sunk when I saw the video. I couldn't believe it. It was awful finding out that our relationship was over.

But the aftermath was worse. The constant whispers, the looks of pity, the giggling, the keyboard commentators on my life. And there was nothing I could do. The joys of social media and all that. Once it's out there, it never goes away. It went viral."

"Fuck, no wonder social media makes you anxious. I'm so sorry, sweetheart. That's not something you should have had to deal with. I hate that he did that to you. But I can't help but be a little grateful." Tracing soft circles on her hand, I feel her tense at the last confession.

Her head snaps up in shock. "Grateful?"

"Yeah. If he hadn't been such a colossal asshole, then you wouldn't be here now. And the selfish bastard that I am, is really happy that you are." I send her a cheeky smile and she laughs, the sound causing heat to radiate in my chest.

"I guess everything does happen for a reason, right?" A small smile graces her face. Not her usual light up the room smile, but a smile nonetheless, and that makes me far happier than it should.

"So they say. Though I've never really believed it until now," I say, pushing a strand of hair behind her ear and tilting her chin up so she's facing me. All rational thought leaves me. The world fades away and it's just the two of us. "He never deserved you."

Leaning forward, I kiss her like she deserves to be kissed. By a man that sees what a gift she is.

CHAPTER TWELVE

Ollie

After our kiss last night, we talked and talked until her eyes kept drifting shut. I didn't want to push her into something when she's still healing, so I said goodnight like a gentleman and we went our separate ways.

Sleep eluded me most of the night, so I made myself a coffee and sat out on the bottom step of the porch staircase, ready to witness the sunrise. The pinks and oranges are breath-taking. This here is one of my favourite things. The peacefulness of the location, the hope of a new day.

I hear her before I see her. The screen door opens and closes and the creaky boards of the porch tell me she's at the top of the stairs. The hairs on the back of my neck stand up in awareness, and I feel my heartrate pick up.

"Morning," I say, turning to smile up at her. With her blonde hair loose, blowing in the slight breeze and her eyes fixated on the ocean, she looks carefree. Beautiful.

She snaps out of her trance and looks down at me with a shy smile.

"Morning, sorry to interrupt." In her pale blue sundress, she looks like an angel standing at the top of the stairs looking down to where I'm perched.

"Not at all." Standing, I make my way up the stairs toward her. "If I'm up early enough, I like to sit out here and watch the sunrise."

"It's so peaceful here. I can see why you love it," she says, leaning against the railing and taking a sip of her coffee. The soft fabric of her dress rides up as she leans over the railing and I advert my eyes, not wanting to wake my cock up this early.

"Gram used to sit out here and watch the sun come up. I used to set my alarm to come down and sit with her. She said it was a healing process. To see a new beginning, the start of a new day. To know that what happened yesterday is now in the past and today you can write a new chapter in your story."

"I like the sound of that. She sounds like an amazing woman," Charlotte says, smiling at me over the rim of her coffee mug.

"She really was," I say, smiling at the memory of her

sitting on this porch and telling me about the beach. She had such a zest for life.

"I love the beach. Living in the city, I don't get to see the sea as much as I would like. There's something so calming about it, don't you think?" A soft sigh leaves her lips and I watch her take in the view as if she is committing it all to memory. I take the moment to study her face, her soft lips that were pressed to mine last night. I know I'm crossing a line. But I really can't bring myself to stop.

"I do. Gram used to have this theory." I chuckle at the passion with which she'd tell me this. "She said the ocean had healing properties. That if you stand at the edge and feel the tide run up your feet, it's washing away your troubles. She used to say the ocean was listening when you told it your dreams, and they rode in on waves and crashed at your feet on the shore."

"That's a nice thought," Charlotte agrees, taking another sip of her coffee and looking over at the ocean. She looks deep in thought for a moment and I don't interrupt. Finally, she lets out another sigh and says, "I wish it could wash away my anxiety."

Looking over at her again, I really feel for her. She didn't ask for this. She's a wonderful woman who deserves to be happy. Her ex did a number on her, and she hasn't taken the time to heal.

"Why don't we go give it a go?" I ask suddenly, putting my empty mug down on the table and moving to the stairs. She needs to start healing, and I want to be the one to help her.

"What?" Tilting her head at me like I've suddenly

grown another one, she scrunches her nose up in confusion and it's adorable.

"Let's go put our feet in the ocean and see if it heals us," I say, aware of how crazy it sounds, but why the hell not? Gram believed it and she was one of the smartest women I knew.

She looks at me like I'm crazy, but nods and puts her mug down next to mine before following me down the stairs. Once we get to the beach, I take off my sneakers and motion for her to do the same. She rolls her eyes and slips off her sandals, leaving them on the bottom step.

Grabbing her hand, I walk us up to the ocean, where the tide is lapping at the shore. The feel of her soft skin against mine has my pulse racing.

Looking over at her, I say, "Gram used to say that you needed to tell the ocean your troubles, then step into the water to let it wash them away."

She looks sceptical and I chuckle. I do sound crazy, I accept that. But hey, what's a little crazy between friends?

"Come on, sweetheart. Humour me, ok?" Letting go of her hand, I turn to the ocean and let out a breath. "I want to be able to open myself up to people again, without the fear of being taken advantage of or hurt. I want to move forward with my life and stop looking back."

Once I've got that off of my chest, I take a step into the water and bite back a curse at the feel of the cold liquid coating my feet. I smile as it rushes up the beach then falls back, taking my words with it into the vast ocean beyond. I imagine it taking my troubles away like Gram said it would and I smile. I do feel lighter. Granted it is probably in my head, but I'll take it.

Turning to Charlotte, I motion for her to do the same. With a sceptical look which gives way to a small smile, she looks out toward the immense body of water and inhales deeply.

"I want to stop being afraid to live. I want to enjoy my life and not worry about what others think about me. It's exhausting. Hiding away from everything, always being on my guard. I want to be free." She exhales then steps into the water and lets out a small squeal as she feels the cold water around her ankles.

Laughing, I look over to her and smile. She's so much braver than she realises.

"You know, I understand why it makes you anxious. I do. But is it not better to be scared and do something anyway, than live your life hiding away from anything that could hurt you? So what if someone sees a photo of you? So what if someone hears you sing out of tune? Who cares? News flash: no one is perfect, sweetheart. No one."

"You make it sound so reasonable." She attempts a laugh but it sounds feeble, even to me. Her shoulders are hunched as she watches the water.

"I'm not making light of your fears. I get it, truly I do. I just hate to see you hide away from the world when you have so much to offer it. You're so much stronger than you realise." Reaching for her soft hand, I give it a squeeze and enjoy the warmth of it.

"I want to be. I don't want to become a crazy cat lady who avoids everything." She gives me a little laugh, and I smile in return. I run my thumb up and down the back of her palm as we stand on the beach and open up to each other.

"So don't. Let's start small. Let me take you to dinner tomorrow night. A proper date, surrounded by other people. Let me show you that with the right person by your side, it doesn't have to be scary." Looking into her eyes, I see the hesitation, but I also see the hope. She wants to let go and enjoy herself, and I want to be the person who helps her to do that.

"Ok," she says, looking up at me and moving her hair out of her face. The determination filling her gaze surprises me.

"Yeah?" I ask, surprised but ecstatic that she's finally letting me in. I won't let her down.

No, just your best mate...

"Yes. I would love to go on a date with you." She turns to look at the water again and I look at her, really look at her. I'm blown away. She's standing in front of me, with her guard down, and ankle deep in cold water, but she's never looked more beautiful than she does right now. With her hair blowing in the breeze, her cheeks flushed as she stands mesmerized by the ocean, she looks relaxed. It suits her. And I'll do anything to keep it that way.

CHAPTER THIRTEEN

Charlotte

The mess in my bedroom is almost comical. Clothes scattered everywhere, shoes discarded left, right, and centre. Ollie is taking me on a date in less than an hour and I still have no clue what to wear. I'm so out of practice with this. My palms are sweating for crying out loud.

It's just dinner, I remind myself as I take a couple of deep breaths and try to pull myself together. We've spent every day together for the past few weeks, had dinner together, this is no different.

Settling on a pair of jeans and a lilac peplum top, I sit at the dressing table to put my makeup on. Staring at my reflection, I smile. I feel lighter than when I first landed her, freer. Ollie makes me feel human again, he makes me feel desired. I didn't realise how much I had missed that. Things with Carl hadn't been right for a long time before it all went down the toilet. I forgot how nice it felt to be wanted.

Checking the time, I grab my purse and slip my phone and lipstick inside before slipping on my heels and heading downstairs. Ollie must hear me descend as he comes out of the kitchen to meet me. He stops when he sees me, his eyes widening and his smile blinding.

"Wow," he says, with a soft chuckle that has me heating. The butterflies in my stomach are having a rave, and I grip hold of the banister to navigate that last couple of steps.

"You look beautiful," he says as he takes my hand and kisses my knuckles.

"Thank you. You look pretty handsome yourself," I say, with a smile. In dark blue jeans and a pale blue shirt rolled up at the sleeves, his ink still on display, he looks like he should be modelling for a calendar.

"You ready to go?" His confidence is reassuring. I'm glad one of us has it. The thought of being in a restaurant with God knows how many other people has my palms sweating and my mouth drying out. But Ollie's right. I can do this, with him to start with. But I'm a strong woman. I can beat this phobia of mine, I don't have to let it define me.

"As ready as I'll ever be." Taking a deep breath, I follow him to the door, watching as he swipes his truck keys from the entryway table. He sure knows how to fill out those jeans. I can't take my eyes away from his backside.

"It'll be fine, I promise. Just relax and focus on what great company I am." He turns and says with a wink, and I playfully shove his chest as he opens the door and leads me out.

Once I've climbed into the truck, I turn to him and ask, "Where are we going?"

"*Steak Out.* It's this steakhouse that has the most amazing view."

"Sounds good." And popular. I bet it is heaving with customers. I cross and uncross my legs, trying to get comfortable and take my mind off of my fears, and Ollie is quick to notice. His hand finds my knee and he gives it a reassuring squeeze.

"Breathe, Charlotte. We're going to have fun, I promise." His tone is comforting and I focus on his words as I take a couple of deep breaths, trying to inhale positivity and exhale negatively. It was in one of the self-help books I bought online back home. Forcing the tightness in my chest to loosen, I give him a small smile and nod. He's right. We will have fun.

***

By the time the waitress brings our main courses out, I am having fun. Conversation flows easily, with Ollie having me in fits of giggles often. Hearing stories about him and my brother in their university days is hilarious. I can't wait to call Alex and make fun of him.

Biting into my sirloin steak, I let out a groan of

appreciation. "Oh, my word. This is incredible."

Ollie's rough chuckle causes warmth to flood my body. I meet his eyes and return his smile.

"I told you, they have the best steak around. Worth every penny."

"What's the plan once the B&B is up and running? Are you going to move in and be the host, or hire someone else to do that and go back to hauling?" It's funny how I've been here for a while, yet this is the first time I've wondered what happens next. After our project is over.

"To be honest I haven't thought that far ahead. I guess I'll hire someone, I'm not the best at being a host." Cutting another chunk of his steak, he slips it into his mouth and savours the rich taste. I find myself following every movement before getting myself under control.

"I don't know. Crappy coffee aside, you've been a great host to me."

That sexy smile of his stretches across his face, and I can feel my heartrate picking up the pace.

"That's because it's you. I'm not like this with everyone."

"Just women?" I tease, tracing my finger along the bottom of my wine glass.

"Just beautiful women with expensive taste in coffee and a love of country music," he jokes, and I feel my face flush. The atmosphere has changed, the chemistry between us sizzling like it could catch fire at any moment. The green in his eyes has darkened and I find myself captivated by his hypnotic gaze.

"I like what I like, I can't help it," I reply with a shrug, as he reaches over and takes my hand in his. The warmth of his touch lighting fireworks in my body.

"Me too, regardless of whether or not it's a good idea." He sighs and offers me a sad smile, his thumbing tracing circles on the back of my hand.

"Because of Alex?"

"Yeah. He's one of my best mates. Rule number one of the bro code, stay away from little sisters." He lets out a humourless chuckle and looks at our entwined hands.

"I love my brother. But I'm an adult. My relationships are none of his business." This is the happiest I've felt in as long as I can remember, and a part of that is down to Ollie. He makes me feel brave, makes me feel like the real me again. I have no idea if this… whatever it is between us has a future. But I know that I want to see what happens.

"I know. But he might not be happy about me dating you. He's really protective over you. Do you know how many times he's called since you arranged to fly over here?" Ollie chuckles, shaking his head. "Not to mention the daily messages I've had since you arrived."

"Yeah, I know. After shit went down with Carl, it's like he's been overcompensating. Like he felt guilty or something, which is ridiculous. But I don't want my brother to dictate my relationships."

"I get that. He means a lot to me. The last thing I want to do is mess up our friendship. But Christ, if I don't spend every waking moment thinking about you. You consume me, Charlotte." That confession has my temperature soaring and I bite my lip to hide my giddy smile. Ollie reaches across and frees it from between my teeth.

"Don't tempt me, sweetheart." He groans, his thumb still on my lip, and I resist the urge to slip it into my mouth. "I'm trying to be a gentleman."

"I didn't ask you to be," I whisper back, sounding breathless even to my own ears. There's something about Ollie that makes me wild, my control evaporates and I'm one hundred percent in the moment.

He pulls back as our waitress comes over to ask how our meal is, making polite small talk while I try to bring my heart rate down to an acceptable level. This is new to me. I've never had such a visceral reaction to someone before. It's like he's the sun and I'm stuck in his orbit, his gravitational pull so strong it throws all reason out of its path.

The conversation stays strictly platonic while we are finishing the last of our meal, which I am grateful for. I'm not ashamed of how I feel, of who I desire, but discussing it in such a public place is still a little uncomfortable.

After settling the bill, Ollie takes my hand in his and leads me to his truck, opening the passenger door for me to hop in. As he slips into the driver's seat, he turns to say something, and I cut him off by pressing my lips to his. I'm not overthinking, not worrying about the consequences. I'm just enjoying the moment, the here and now.

Ollie's tongue runs along my bottom lip and I open my mouth with a gasp, granting him access. My fingers run through his hair, needing him closer. Before I can comprehend what's happening, he's lifted me over the centre console to straddle him, his hands wrapping around my waist.

Groaning into the kiss, I run one hand down his shirt covered torso, and he grabs it before I can reach below the waist.

"Fuck. You make me crazy, sweetheart," he admits, leaning his forehead against mine, his breathing heavy and laboured.

"Is that a bad thing?" I ask with a smile.

"Definitely not a bad thing, but we should head back to the house before I throw you on to the backseat and get arrested for public indecency." His cocky smirk has me biting my lip and muffling a moan of my own. Climbing back into the passenger seat, I check my reflection in the mirror and put my seatbelt on. Ollie starts the truck and pulls out of the car park, slipping his free hand onto my thigh.

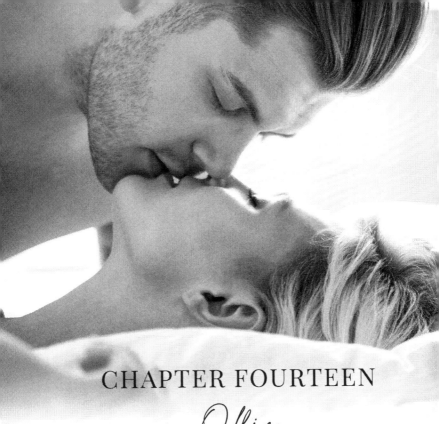

CHAPTER FOURTEEN

Ollie

Charlotte was still dead to the world when I woke this morning, so I thought I'd head out for a run along the beach to wake myself up and get rid of some of the pent up energy. The sea air is refreshing, and the sound of the water always has me forgoing music. This is mother nature's playlist right here.

Our kisses from last night play on repeat through my head. The soft moans she made, the way her fingers gripped my hair, the taste of her. I'm in too deep before I've even begun. As much as I wanted to take her to bed, I'm in no rush. She's worth the wait, and dinner last night was a big step for her. I didn't want to then make her anxious about where we were heading. It was about making her comfortable again, and I hope I managed that.

As the house comes back into view, my phone starts buzzing in my pocket. Slowing to a stop, I pull it out and see Alex's face flash up on the screen. My chest constricts with guilt, but I try to shake the feeling off before answering the call.

"Hey, bud, you ok?" I ask, still out of breath from my early morning exercise.

"Yeah, all good, man. How's everything there, you ok?"

"You called me at 6.30 am to ask how I'm doing?" I chuckle down the phone line, walking back towards the house.

"Shit. Sorry. I suck at time differences."

"It's cool. I was running along the beach to wake myself up."

"How's the house coming along?" he asks.

"Really good. We've done most of the hard work. Just need to look into marketing it now, how to get people through the door, you know?"

"That's awesome. You two have been busy," he says and I freeze. I know he doesn't mean anything by it, but I feel like a snake. He's counting on me to take care of his baby sister, and I'm sure he didn't mean by feeling her up in my truck and playing tonsil tennis with her.

"Yeah, we have," I say, staring down at my feet and grateful he can't see me.

"Send some photos over later, I want to see this DIY masterpiece," he jokes and I agree before we say our goodbyes.

Sitting on the steps of the porch, I look out on the beach and try to remind myself that we're doing nothing wrong. We're two consenting adults, enjoying each other's company. If we're making each other happy, he can't begrudge it, right?

"Hey," a soft voice breaks me out of my thoughts, and I turn to see the object of my thoughts.

"Hey, you ok?" I ask, taking her in. In a pale-yellow skirt and white vest top, barefoot, she looks almost ethereal. Her blonde hair swept to one side and no make-up, she's still a vision.

"Perfect," she says, her cheeks flushing as she no doubt replays last night in her mind like I have been all morning. In the parking lot of the diner, in the truck once we pulled up to the house. Outside her bedroom door before I convinced her to go to bed alone. "Could you not sleep?"

"I had some excess energy to burn off, so thought I'd take a run along the beach." Sending her a playful smirk, I enjoy watching as the flush on her cheeks deepens. The crimson on her cheeks reminds me of a red and cream rose in the sun, striking and special.

Standing, I move up the stairs and stand in front of her, swiping an errant strand of hair from her face enjoying the effect my touch has on her.

"How did you sleep?"

"Like a log." She laughs softly and turns to look at the view. "I had a great time last night. I can't remember if I told you that. I was a bit distracted towards the end of the evening."

Laughing, I pull her closer and tilt her chin so she's facing me.

"Distracted? By our epic makeout session? Or how I insisted we went to bed alone?" I tease, watching with rapt attention as she bites her lip. My blood rushes south and I try to calm myself down.

"Both?" she admits with another soft laugh, and I cut it off by pressing my lips to hers. I could live off of the taste of her. It's decadent and delicious. One hundred percent Charlotte, and I don't think I'll ever get enough. Her arms wrap around my neck as she deepens the kiss, and I groan into her mouth.

"You're addictive, you know that?" I ask against her lips as she pulls back to take a breath.

"You taste like coffee, and Ollie, it's kinda making me jealous."

A rough laugh rumbles out of me and I pull her in for another kiss.

"Come on, fiend. Let's get you caffeinated." With one last look over my shoulder at the ocean, I smile to Gram, knowing she's out there, and lead Charlotte inside.

CHAPTER FIFTEEN

Charlotte

Watching Ollie lay out all of the ingredients for his Gram's famous take on Snickerdoodles, I wonder if this is such a good idea. We've spent days cleaning and decorating, do we really want to ruin all our hard work with my terrible kitchen skills?

"So this is everything we need. I've put the oven on to preheat, ok?" he asks, looking over at me with a delicious smile. "You ready to see the magic happen?"

A laugh escapes me at his excited expression. He seems

so relaxed and carefree in the kitchen. It's nice to see him have fun and not worry about money or getting this place up and running. As the weeks have passed, I feel like we've both opened up more.

"As ready as I'll ever be. I will warn you again though, I am awful in the kitchen. Truly terrible." I'm not sure he fully understands just how bad I am. I burn everything. Pasta, toast, you name it, I've ruined it.

"I'm a great teacher, trust me. You're in good hands." My eyes dart to said hands and I can't help but agree. I bet they'd feel really good running along my…

"So to start, we weigh out all the ingredients. We need three cups of flour." He breaks me out of my indecent thoughts and I hope my blush doesn't give me away.

"Three cups? What's a cup?" Does he use mugs to measure ingredients? That seems odd.

He pulls a cup from one of the drawers and I see what it is. "Oh, you mean a scoop. Why don't you just measure it? Use the scale to work out how many grams you need."

"Because this is America, sweetheart. They don't use your weird measurements, they use cups." He stage-sighs as if I'm completely inept, and he isn't far wrong but I grin anyway.

Laughing, I shake my head. "Whatever you say, oh wise one."

The scowl that appears on his face aimed at me makes me laugh harder, until I feel something hit me.

What the…?

"Did you just throw a scoop of flour at me?" I ask, taken aback.

"Nope. I threw a *cup* of flour at you." He has a smug grin on his face, and I'm torn between wanting to kiss it off him and wanting to retaliate.

Retaliation wins. I rush forward and grab the bag of flour, burying my hand inside and pulling out a handful of flour which I launch in his direction. It hits him in the face and I don't believe it. My aim is shocking, how on earth I got a direct bullseye, I have no idea. I throw my head back and laugh. Full on belly laugh like I haven't in so long.

"You think that's funny, huh?" he asks, but I'm too busy holding my stomach so I don't keel over from laughing so hard. He looks like Casper the ghost.

I hear the crack before I feel the wetness seeping down my neck. Snapping my head up, I look at him. "Did you just crack an egg on my head?"

The smug smile is back and now he's the one laughing. Looking for some more ammunition, I settle on the glass of water on the side. Picking it up, I swing around and throw it at him, drenching his shirt. His gasp of surprise makes me proud, but then he launches forward and grabs me, getting me wet too. With his arms wrapped around me, he pulls me with him as he grabs some cinnamon and sprinkles it over my head. I'm in hysterics now, this is crazy. But it's the most fun I've had in as long as I can remember.

Flinging my arms to the counter, I grab the bag of flour and toss more over him, laughing as he pulls back with a shout.

"Now you're asking for it," he says, wiping flour from his face and laughing at the state of us. His green eyes sparkle with mischief, and I suck in a breath at how his shirt is sticking to his chest, highlighting his insane physique.

"You started it!" I say, looking around the kitchen at the mess we've made.

Woops.

Turning back to him, I watch as he runs a finger through the readymade chocolate frosting.

"I did. And I'm going to finish it," he says, stepping toward me with his finger outstretched. I step back and bump into the counter, letting him box me in. He uses his finger to trace my lips, and I see his pupils dilate in hunger which I assume has nothing to do with the frosting.

Leaning forward, he crashes his lips to mine. The combined taste of him and the chocolate frosting has me moaning into his mouth. It tastes out of this world. I wrap my arms around his neck and pull him closer, enjoying the moment. His kisses should come with a warning. They leave you craving more, desperate for another taste.

"Fuck, sweetheart. You're the best snickerdoodle I've ever tasted," he jokes with a groan before claiming my lips again. The feel of his strong arms wrapped around my waist sends shivers up my spine. He makes me feel safe and free at the same time and I love it.

"We should probably jump in the shower and clean this mess up," I say, looking around as I pull back breathlessly. I don't want to break the kiss, but I'm covered in flour and raw egg, it's hardly appetising.

"You're right, come on." Grabbing my hand in his, he leads me up the stairs and to his master bedroom. I follow him into his en suite as he opens the sliding doors to the shower and turns the water on. "You go first, this is the nicest shower in the house," he says, as he turns to leave.

I have no idea where my newfound confidence comes from, but I grasp his hand before he can leave. The feel of his skin on mine is electrifying. My thoughts may be in overdrive, but right now the one that is screaming the loudest is that I don't want this moment to end yet.

"Do you think you could help me wash my back?" I ask, feeling the colour drench my cheeks but maintaining eye contact. I know what I want. It's him.

A sinful smile spreads across his handsome face as he steps toward me. "Is that what you want?" The husky tone to his voice has me clenching my thighs together in need.

"More than snickerdoodles," I say and he laughs, pulling his flour covered t-shirt over his head and dropping it onto the tiled floor. His chest is a work of art. With toned abs and the gorgeous tattoo on his right arm, I'm momentarily awestruck. Forget snickerdoodles, I want to eat him.

"In that case, let's get wet," he says with a cocky grin that does things to my insides. Pulling my long shirt over my head, I throw it down with his and lean over to pull my leggings down. By the time I'm done, he's already standing in front of me, naked as the day he was born. And my word, Ollie is packing.

"Shall we?" he grins, catching me staring at his impressive 'utensil' and motioning to the shower. I climb in and sigh as the warm water hits my body and relaxes me. I feel his body slide up against mine as he pulls the shower doors closed behind us. I'm on fire and a cold shower won't cure me. It's him. I'm desperate for him. The butterflies in my stomach are on steroids, fluttering up a storm, and my pulse is racing.

Reaching for the shampoo, I squeeze a dollop into my hand and start massaging it into my egg filled locks. He reaches around me for the body wash and whispers in my ear, "Do you mind if I help?"

Shivers dance along my spine at his words and the feel of his breath on my skin. I have no idea how we ended up here, but I'll be damned if I'm not going to enjoy every second of it.

"Be my guest," I say, turning and leaning my head under the shower head to remove the shampoo from my hair. I watch as he pours a generous amount of body wash into his hand and replaces the bottle on the shelf. Then he's reaching out and running his strong hands down my torso. His touch sets me alight. I feel things I haven't felt in so long. As he reaches my breasts, he cups them in his strong hands and squeezes, eliciting a strangled moan from me.

"Fuck, Ollie," I whimper, using my hands to trace the lines of his sculpted torso. He is both hard and soft at the same time, strong and supple. I lick my lips at the sight of his hard erection standing proudly to attention before me. I trace a hand slowly down his happy trail before I reach the treasure that is his cock. Taking it in my hand, I enjoy the weight of it as I gently squeeze. He throws his head back and groans.

"Keep that up and this won't last long, sweetheart." He sighs in pleasure and I smile that I caused that pleasure. I let go and trail my hands back up his chest, standing on tiptoes and kissing him again. His arms wrap around me and the feel of his hard length between us has me moaning. I need him more than I need my next breath.

Pulling away, he holds me at arm's length, and I frown in confusion.

"I want to look at you," he whispers in his deep voice and I feel goose bumps spread all over my body. The hunger and desire in his eyes has me flushing. He takes his time, studying every inch of my body with a lustful expression. "Fucking perfect."

Smiling, I take his hand and press it against my stomach, slowly leading it down to where I want him most. He picks up on my plan quickly and takes control, his deft fingers finding my clit and drawing circles around it, toying with me.

"Ollie. Please," I whimper, leaning back against the tiled wall of the shower and biting my lip to contain my moans.

He removes his hand and my eyes fly open in disappointment which causes him to chuckle at my reaction.

"We are nowhere near done, sweetheart. But I don't want our first time to be in the shower. Let's take this to the bedroom." He holds his hand out and I take it, letting him help me step out of the shower. He lets go of my hand to grab a fluffy white towel which he holds out for me. Wrapping it around myself, I watch fascinated as he takes another towel and makes quick work of drying off his godlike physique.

Could this man be any hotter?

Following his lead, I quickly towel dry as much of myself as I can, eager to get back to our previous activity. Squeezing my blonde locks into the towel, I look up to see him staring at my breasts in hunger. How one hungry gaze can make me feel like a supermodel, I don't know. All I know is that this man affects me like no other. I've never craved someone's touch the way I do his. His kisses are like a cool glass of wine on a hot summer day: delicious, refreshing, and leaves you craving another taste.

"Bedroom. Now," he growls, and damn if I don't need to dry myself off again.

CHAPTER SIXTEEN

Ollie

Looking down at the goddess laid out before me, I thank my lucky stars that she's here. In my life, in my bed. Charlotte came into my life like a tidal wave. That couldn't be a more apt metaphor since tidal waves are caused by the effects of the gravitational pull between the sun, moon, and Earth. And this woman is definitely swiftly becoming both the sun and moon in my life. Lighting up even the darkest of nights and basking me in her glow.

Crawling up her body, I lean down to take her lips with

mine. I'm addicted to the taste of her, the feel of her skin on mine, the sounds she makes when I give her pleasure. She is my addiction and I don't ever want to recover.

Balancing my weight on one forearm, my other hand traces its way down her body and pinches a nipple. The moan of pleasure she elicits almost undoes me. I continue my quest until I reach her wet pussy. Slipping a finger inside, I watch her face as I slowly move in and out. She's biting her lip and it makes me jealous, so I lean forward and do just that. Taking her lip between my teeth and gently biting down, listening to her sharp intake of breath and the breathy moan that follows. I slip another finger inside her and watch captivated as she starts to ride my hand.

"Ollie," she cries as I push her further and further toward her climax. "So close."

Increasing the speed and leaning down to capture a nipple in my mouth, I gently bite down and feel her body convulse under me as the wave crashes over her. Looking up, I take in her expression, could she be any more beautiful?

"Wow," she gasps, closing her eyes and flinging a hand over her face. Laughing, I lean forward and drop a soft kiss to her lips.

"Yeah, you could say that." I chuckle into her mouth. "Watching you come undone may be my new favourite view."

"Please." She laughs before pushing me back and sitting up. "My turn."

Pushing me onto the bed beside her, she throws her leg over my waist and straddles me. As she kisses down my chest, I close my eyes and hum in pleasure at the feel of her soft lips on my skin. I'm on fire, every touch heating my blood like I'm a volcano about to erupt. I feel her shimmying backwards, and my eyes fly open when she wraps her lips around my straining cock. I wrap a hand around her hair and help guide her movements. The feel of her warm mouth around me has me close to the edge and when she adds her tongue... fuck, I'm about to embarrass myself.

"Sweetheart, if you don't stop now, I'm going to explode," I pant as I look down and watch her head bobbing up and down enthusiastically. She looks up at me through her gorgeous long lashes and winks. Throwing my head back against the pillow, I succumb to the pleasure, gripping her hair tighter as I feel my release coming. I shoot my load down her throat and watch captivated as she swallows everything I have to give her.

As she pulls back, I smile and pull her up to kiss me.

"I really want to make a joke about icing the snickerdoodle, but I'm biting my tongue," she says into my chest and I laugh, pulling her to lie against me. My hand snakes down her body to squeeze her arse. Her soft gasp fans over my chest, causing goose bumps to spread across my skin.

"Again?" She giggles into me, looking up at me with a sinful smile that has me craving her mouth again.

"Again. I haven't had my fill of you yet, sweetheart," I say against her lips as she climbs up to kiss me. "Not even close."

Once I've explored her mouth again, memorising every moan and gasp that leaves her, I flip us over so she's on her back and I'm propped above her on my forearms.

Trailing my lips from her collarbone, down to her breasts, I lick and nip at every inch of skin I come into contact with. She writhes beneath me and it spurs me on in my quest to make her scream my name. Moving further south, I kiss her stomach, her hips, her thighs, before running my nose along her inner thighs and smirking when she spreads herself wider with a soft moan. Taking the hint, I situate myself between her legs and stroke her entrance again, watching her squirm with pleasure, still sensitive from her earlier climax.

"Ollie," she moans on a soft whisper, and it's not enough. I want her to lose control. I want her to be so consumed by pleasure that she loses herself to the moment.

My tongue slowly traces her wet lips and she throws her head back, pushing herself further into me. Slipping my tongue into her heat, I savour every taste of her. Enjoy every moan, every groan, and every scrape of her nails on my head.

"Fuck, please," she begs, pushing my head further into her thighs and bucking up, desperate for a release. My movements become faster, more determined. Finding her sweet spot, I focus all my attention on getting her to where she wants to be. Her pleas have become strings of nonsensical sounds, her head thrashing on my pillow as she finds her release and screams my name.

Pulling back, I take a breath and watch her. Lying on my bed, taking deep breaths, looking like a satisfied kitten, the pride that fills my chest is intense.

Reaching into my beside drawer, I pull out a condom and see her eyes follow the movement.

"Again?" she asks, breathless.

"Third times the charm, right?" I joke, smiling so hard I'm sure I seem unhinged. But my god, she is something else.

"You tell me." Biting her lip like a temptress, she spreads her legs again and reaches for me. Sheathing myself in latex, I slip between her thighs and lean over her, kissing her swollen lips.

"Ready?" I ask, moving a damp strand of hair from her flushed face.

"Always. Please," she whispers against my lips.

Sliding inside her, I groan. She's fucking perfect. And right now, she's all mine.

CHAPTER SEVENTEEN

Ollie

The house is really coming together. Charlotte has a great eye and between the two of us, we've done a pretty good job. It was hard at first, changing things that reminded me of my grandparents. But I think they'd approve. The house has a new lease of life and is ready for more people to create magical memories in.

Emptying the last couple of plates from the dishwasher, I hear a knock at the door followed by Charlotte's footsteps.

"I'll get it," she calls and I suspect it's the new bed linen we ordered getting delivered. As I close the dishwasher and start the coffee machine up, I hear a commotion by the door.

"Who the fuck are you?" I recognise the nasally voice instantly and feel ice filling my veins. *How is she here?*

Moving quickly, I enter the foyer and pull the door wider to reveal my ex, staring Charlotte down in disdain. In skinny jeans and a blue halter neck top, she stands on the doorstep with her hands on her hips and attitude in spades. Her gaze flicks to me and she softens, her mask back in place.

"Ollie, baby. I missed you so much," she coos, and I have to clench my fists to keep my temper in check. She's got some fucking nerve coming here.

"What are you doing here, Becky?" Instinctively I want to push Charlotte behind me, not wanting any of Becky's poison to touch her.

She looks taken back by my cold tone, and I try not to let a bitter laugh slip past my pursed lips. Did she really think I'd welcome her back into my life with open arms after what she did?

"I heard you were here. I came to see you. I missed you," she says like it's the most obvious thing in the world. Like we didn't have a nasty breakup.

"Missed me, or my credit cards?" Charlotte shifts uncomfortably next to me, and I put a comforting hand on her back.

"Don't be like that, Ollie. We were good together. We hit a little bump, but that's water under the bridge now. Just tell your little friend to get lost, and we can talk."

"Charlotte's not going anywhere. You are. You're not

welcome here," I seethe. She's out of her mind if she thinks we have anything left to talk about. I'm still paying off the debts she left me in.

Her calm façade turns in an instant, a scowl marring her face. "Are you fucking her?"

Charlotte blanches at the accusation, stiffening beside me, and I'm done. Enough is enough.

"You lost the right to dictate who I can and can't see when you ran up my credit cards and left me once the money dried up. What? Now you heard about this place and thought you'd work your way back into my life to try and get a quick payday from it? We're done, Becky. Leave and never come back." Stepping back, I slam the door in her face, finding it way more satisfying than I should.

Turning to Charlotte, I cup her cheek and tilt her face to look at me. The sadness in her baby blues is my undoing. I lean forward and press my lips to hers, swiping my tongue along her bottom lip before slipping in between them. Her soft moan has my cock waking up and I reluctantly pull back. Now isn't the time.

"Sorry about that. I have no idea how she found out about this place, but she's toxic. Ignore her." Stroking her cheek, I lean my forehead against hers and inhale her sweet scent, attempting to calm my racing pulse.

Charlotte wraps her arms around me and sinks into my embrace. The warmth from her body thaws the ice that Becky's appearance created.

"Are you ok?" Her whispered question has me chuckling, the movement causing her to bounce against her chest.

"You're asking me that? After she blindsided you and was a complete bitch?"

"Well, yeah. She's your ex. I know she hurt you. Seeing her show up her can't have been a nice feeling." Once again, this woman astounds me. Her concern for everyone else before herself once again shows me just how different from Becky she is. I know she'd never betray me like my ex did.

"I'm good. You're here. And we have Snickerdoodles." Her eyes meet mine and the blush that colours her cheeks has me chuckling before I kiss her again.

CHAPTER EIGHTEEN

Charlotte

The afternoon sun is shining in through the bedroom window, covering us in its warm glow. I can't bring myself to move from where I'm curled into Ollie's side. After hands down, the best sex of my life, I don't think I can move even if I wanted to.

Tracing the tattoo on his arm, I look at the intricate design and smile. It's beautiful. The black ink is striking against his soft skin and I run my fingers over it.

"What made you get this?" I ask him, following the

hourglass floating in the sea with my finger and reading the quote inside it. 'Time waits for no man.'

"I got it after I lost Pops. He always used to say this, all the time. He'd say, why put off tomorrow what you can do today? He was a big believer in living in the moment and never wasting a second of the time you are given. The hourglass is to remind me that time isn't permanent, the waves are to remind me of Gram and her love of the ocean. Her belief that it could heal you. Guess the tattoo just makes me feel a little closer to them, you know?"

My heart squeezes in my chest at his words. I can't imagine the grief he must have felt when he lost them, it sounds as if they were so close. Then to be betrayed by the one person he opened himself up to after his loss. My heart breaks for him, and I relax into the warmth his body brings.

"I wish I could have met them. They sound amazing," I say honestly, my fingers still tracing the ink.

"They were. And Gram would have loved you." He chuckles, stroking my hair.

"Do you think so?" The thought warms me as I curl closer to him. I want to know him, inside out. I've never been a big believer in fate, but I do believe it brought me here, to him.

"Are you kidding? Fresh meat to mould in the kitchen? You would have been the dream." Slapping his chest, I laugh as he pulls me onto his chest, curling a hand in my hair and bringing me down to him for a hard kiss.

The ringing of the doorbell has me pulling back, while Ollie throws his head back on the pillow with a groan. Laughing, I climb off of him, squealing when he smacks my bum.

"Behave. That'll be the bed linen. Ready to play maid?" I joke as I pull his shirt over my head and slip my knickers on.

"That depends, can we play dress up?"

His salacious grin has me squeezing my thighs together, as I roll my eyes.

"Mind out of the gutter, Oliver. Let's get to work." Heading out of the room, I look over my shoulder at the Adonis on the bed and offer him a cheeky wink before sauntering off.

"Yes, ma'am."

CHAPTER NINETEEN

Ollie

The house is almost done. It looks worlds away from when Charlotte first arrived. It's modern and elegant and perfect. Sitting on the porch, we're brainstorming how to get it open for business and how to attract guests. I don't think I ever realised how much work would go into getting this place up and running.

Taking a mouthful of coffee, I turn to look out at the beach. There are barely any clouds in the sky, the sun shining on the water creating a myriad of blues dancing with the waves.

"We need to make a website. We'll take some pictures. It's a good way to be seen," Charlotte says, bringing me back to the job at hand, as she scribbles away in a notebook.

"I like that idea. And we can set up some social media accounts too, to get the word out there about the place."

I notice her shift uncomfortably in her seat, the mention of social media triggering her anxiety. I reach across and grab her hand, running my thumb over her soft knuckles before placing a kiss on her palm.

"I'll sort all that, don't worry."

She sends me a grateful smile and it makes me feel ten feet tall. Making her smile has become a favourite hobby of mine. That and getting her naked.

"Ooh, and you need a name! Something cute, that people will remember."

"A name?"

"Yeah like, Memories and Muffins, or Sun, Sand, and Sleep." The fact that she says those with a straight face blows my mind.

"You know they're terrible right?" I laugh at her affronted expression and pull her head down to kiss her hair.

"They were just examples, you arse. You get the idea though." She slaps my chest but leans into my hold nonetheless.

"Yeah, loud and clear." Scouring my brain to come up with something, I look out to the beach again "Beach B&B?" I offer, but I can see from her look of disdain that I didn't pass the test.

"That is awful." We're both laughing now, and I wish

I could capture her now on camera. Her cheeks are flushed from laughing, her hair is loose and pushed over one shoulder. And she looks happy.

"How about Ocean Dreams?" she offers and I pause to think.

"I like that. Let's roll with it." Her smile lights up the room as she writes in down and we go back to brainstorming ways to get the word out about the place.

"Maybe you should sign up to be on one of those B&B reality shows. You know the one where owners take it in turns to stay at each other's places?" she jokes, trying to lighten the mood.

"Now there's an idea. I can charm everyone with my amazing personality and quick wit." I waggle my eyebrows at her and she snorts.

"They don't always come out looking great." She rolls her eyes and goes back to writing notes.

I shrug with a smile. "No such thing as bad publicity, right? Anything that gets our name out there is worth doing."

"I guess so," she agrees before picking up her coffee and looking out to the water. After a short period of comfortable silence, she turns back to me. "I feel lighter, you know? Like I'm finally moving on and letting go of my fears."

"See, and you thought Gram was crazy claiming the ocean could heal you." I laugh, but she shakes her head with a smile.

"I don't think it's the ocean. It's you," she whispers, the emotion in her eyes taking my breath away. Reaching across, I pull her to me, sealing my lips over hers and showing her how much she has come to mean to me.

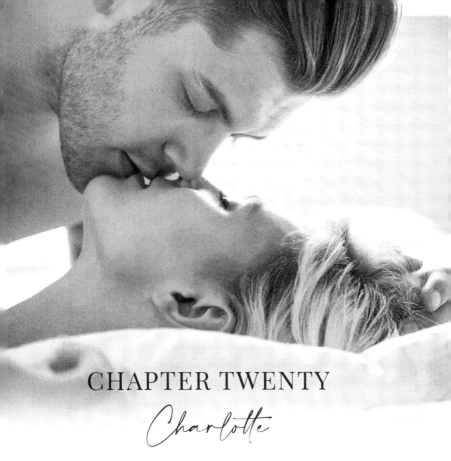

CHAPTER TWENTY

Charlotte

When Melody called and asked if I wanted to meet for coffee, I can't say I wasn't surprised. But I agreed, looking forward to getting to know Ollie's friends a little better.

She stands and waves as I walk in, gesturing to the coffee on the table she's already ordered for me.

"Charlotte, I'm so glad you came," she says, pulling me in for a friendly hug.

"Thanks for asking me. Other than Ollie, I don't know

anyone here."

"That's because he's been keeping you all to himself," she jokes and I laugh, taking a seat across from her and thanking her for my drink.

"What brings you to this neck of the woods? Don't you guys live quite a way away?" I take a sip of my coffee and sigh at the rich taste hitting my tongue.

"Yeah, Scott was passing through for work anyway, so I asked if he minded dropping me off on his way. Figured we could use some girl talk, then I can get some shopping done before he picks me up on his way back through."

"Is it tough? Having his job taking him away so much?" I ask, genuinely curious. I don't know if I could cope with my other half being away at night or for days at a time. But maybe that's because of how things with Carl turned out.

"It can be. But Scott is careful never to take anything too far that will keep him away for too long. And on trips like this, if I'm not working, I tag along." Her smile is infectious and I know that I could be great friends with her. She's the kind of girl you want on your team. Confident, loyal, and fun to be around.

"How is the house coming along?" she asks, before she takes another mouthful of her tea.

"Good. We're looking into marketing now, how to get the word out that people can book rooms in the next couple of months." I'm ridiculously proud of what we've achieved. Granted we only made superficial changes, but we gave the house a new lease of life.

"We'll have to come by and see it soon. Maybe we can test it out for the first time." Her sweet laugh has me smiling, nodding in agreement.

"You totally should. That would be fun. I know Ollie misses you guys." He talks about them with such a fondness, it's impossible not to see how much they mean to him.

"Yeah, he had it rough for a while, but he seems to be picking himself back up. I think we have you to thank for that," Melody teases, clearly looking for gossip and to my surprise, that doesn't fill me with dread. There's no invisible force tightening in my chest, not sweaty palms or nausea swirling in my stomach.

"I don't think it's down to me. I think renovating his grandparents' house has been cathartic for him. Helped him to move on and see the bigger picture, you know?"

"Yeah. He seems more like himself. What about you? Are you planning on hanging around once the house is done, or do you have plans back in the UK?"

The question is innocent enough but makes me pause. Truth be told, I haven't thought much about what happens once the house is finished. I've been too busy living in the moment to worry about the future. And I like it. I like taking each day as it comes, not worrying about where I'm going or what the future holds. It's refreshing and freeing.

"I don't really know, to be honest. I came here to get away from all the crap I was going through back home. I feel like I've done that. But I don't know if I'm ready to go back." Will this new version of me disappear as soon as I set foot back in England?

"I'm aware that I am an incredible nosey nelly, but can I ask what happened?" Her expression is almost apologetic, and it makes me smile.

A laugh leaves my lips at her admission. "Bad break up. Really bad. And my anxiety kind of got the better of me, going out in public, social media, it all became a bit too much, you know? I just wanted to hide away from everything and everyone. But I think I'm done hiding now."

"Good for you, sweetie."

Her hand reaches across the table and squeezes mine, and just like that, I know I've made a true friend.

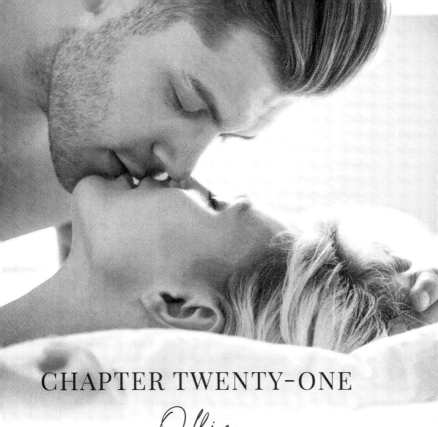

CHAPTER TWENTY-ONE

Ollie

Picnics have never really been my thing, but sitting on the beach on a blanket with Charlotte, watching the sunset, I sure as hell can't complain.

Granted, ordering takeaway pizza might be cheating, but the sentiment is the same. Taking a slug of my cold beer, I smile down at where Charlotte's head is resting on my lap. She's watching the waves crashing on the shore with a smile, both of us enjoying the peace of the night.

"Do you know what blows my mind? Clouds." She's

twirling a strand of her blonde hair around her finger and looking curiously up at the sky.

"Clouds?" I ask, both confused and amused by this.

"Yeah. They look like candy floss, right? Soft and airy. But did you know they're really heavy? One can weigh like one million pounds. And they still float in the sky above us, acting harmless." Her lips have formed a pout, and she looks perturbed by the thought.

I stifle a laugh, playing with her hair. "They *are* harmless. I've never heard of death by cloud, have you?"

"No but maybe it's covered up, you know? So people don't panic about the floating death pillows in the air." She thrusts her arm in the air, motioning to the clouds in the sky.

Throwing my head back, I can no longer hold back my laughter. Where does she get this shit from?

"You're insane, you know that, right?"

She sits up and looks at me with an adorable pout on her face that I'm sorely tempted to kiss off. I settle for sweeping her hair behind her ear, enjoying the way she leans into my touch.

"I'm not. It's a valid concern. How are they still floating in the air if they weigh the same as one hundred elephants?"

"How can an aeroplane stay in the air with how much it weighs?" I counter, because that's also incredible.

She scoffs. "Don't get me started on those death traps, they…"

Cutting her off, I press my lips to hers, wrapping my fingers in her hair and pulling her closer. The sweet taste of the fruity wine on her tongue combined with her intoxicating flavour has me groaning. She shifts so she's straddling me, her fingers in my hair, pulling me in, like she can't get close enough, and I know the feeling.

Moving my hand up to underneath her shirt, I stroke the soft skin beneath it and feel her tremble in my arms. Her skin is smooth as silk, and one touch leaves me craving more. I want to take her inside and worship every inch of her.

Charlotte pulls back, smiling up at me before snuggling into my chest. Dropping a kiss on her head, I look out to the ocean and watch the swells of water sweep towards us.

"I'm really glad you came here," I whisper into her hair.

"Me too," she whispers back, leaning closer and watching the water dance in the soft light of the evening.

We need to talk about the future. About how we'll handle things with her brother, and what the plan is once the B&B opens. But for now, none of that matters. All that does is that we're both here, in the moment, together.

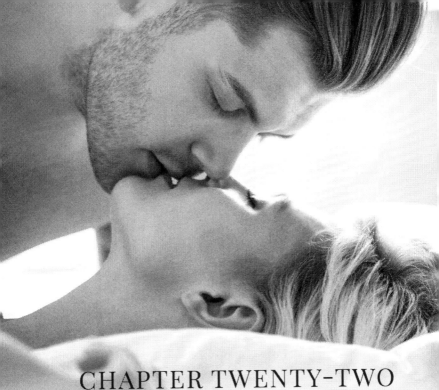

CHAPTER TWENTY-TWO

Charlotte

Loading the washing machine, I spin around to the cupboard under the sink and get the washing detergent. Before I can add it to the machine, my phone buzzes on the table. My brother's face flashes up on the screen and I smile, accepting the video call.

"Hey, Lottie," Alex says as his face fills my screen. His brown hair wet and stuck to his face.

"Hey! You just got out of the shower?" I ask, grabbing my coffee and heading to the porch.

"I wish. Just been for a run, and it absolutely pissed it down!" he admits, running his fingers through his wet hair.

"I definitely don't miss the weather." I laugh, flipping the camera to show him the beach with the sun boring down on it.

"Alright, show off. I get it." He laughs and I flip the camera back to me, smiling at him. "Still enjoying yourself?"

The guilt gnawing at my gut has me squeezing my fist together as I answer. I hate keeping things from my brother, but I don't want to ruin this.

"Yes. The house is almost ready. Ollie's friends are coming over tomorrow to be the first guests. A little trial run kinda thing. The website is up, and we got him listed on a few holiday home search engines. So fingers crossed."

"Woah. You guys have sure been busy." *You have no idea.*

"Yeah. But it's come out great, and I think it's going to do well."

"Good. And how are you? Ready to come home?"

I pause, looking down and must give myself away.

"Lot? What's up?" he asks, his soothing tone my undoing.

"I'm thinking of staying," I admit, for the first time aloud.

"What?"

"I really like it here. And I'm doing so much better. I was thinking of asking Ollie if I could stay and host the B&B for a while, just until it gets on its feet, you know?"

"Really? What did Ollie say?" he asks, remaining calmer than I expected.

"I haven't actually discussed it with him yet. I've been thinking on it a lot. Still haven't made a firm choice, but it's an option I'm considering." I feel lighter for voicing it. Truth be told, I've been thinking about staying a lot recently.

"You know I just want you to be happy, Lot. If staying over there makes you happy, then I'm all for it." The sincerity in his eyes guts me. He's always been my biggest supporter, protector, and champion. And I'm lying to him.

"Thank you. I love you," I say, sticking my tongue out at him like I used to when we were kids.

His soft laugh flows through my phone speaker. "Love you too, sis."

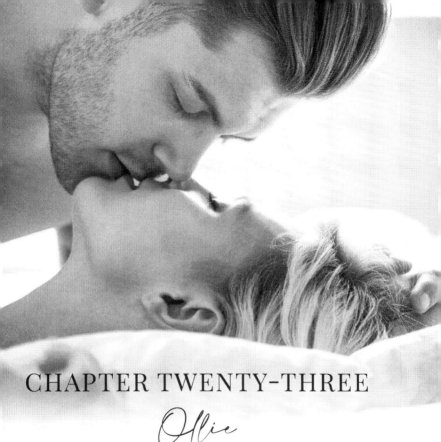

CHAPTER TWENTY-THREE

Ollie

The doorbell rings and Charlotte ducks past me to get it. We haven't officially opened yet, but tonight we are welcoming our first guests.

Scott and Melody.

"Hello, and welcome to Ocean Dreams," Charlotte says, as she motions for the couple to enter. I try not to chuckle at her, but Scott and Melody indulge her little role play.

"Hey, man, place looks good," Scott says as he approaches me and bumps my fist.

"Thanks, bud. And thanks for offering to try the place out. Charlotte's been beyond excited to take the place for a test run," I say as he chuckles and looks over to where the two women are catching up like old friends.

"Like I had a choice. Melody all but dragged me out of the house. She's been dying to see the place." Just as the woman in question walks toward us and gives me a quick hug.

"Well, duh. The photos looked amazing, and that view?" She whistles. "It's going to be popular, that's for sure. Had to book while we still had the chance."

Charlotte is quick to offer a tour of the house and show them to their room. She seems to enjoy playing hostess, and I wonder whether it's something she'd be interested in. We haven't spoken about what she's going to do when this place is done. I'm hoping she wants to stay, but if she wants to go home, I'd understand. Her whole life is back in the UK. I can't just ask her to leave it all behind to stay with me. Especially as we've never discussed the future.

"I've gotta admit it, man, you've done an awesome job. Didn't know you had it in you," Scott says, lifting his beer to his lips as he looks over the porch railing at the beach. Charlotte and Melody are walking along the waterfront, talking about God knows what.

"Most of it was Charlotte. She's got a great eye," I admit, taking a swig of my own beer and watching the women enjoying the beach.

"How're things going with the two of you?" he asks, looking at me over his beer bottle.

"Good. Great. She's…" I trail off, watching her laughing

at something Melody has told her, her bare feet wading in the water. Soft hair blowing in the breeze and not a care in the world. My chest swells at the sight. In such a short space of time, she's become so important to me.

"Dude? Where'd you go?" Scott asks with a chuckle, following my gaze. "*Really* good then?"

"Yeah. But it's complicated." Rubbing a hand over my face, I sigh and lean against the railing on my forearms. I should have told Alex as soon as things began. The longer we've let it go on without telling him, the deeper my betrayal has become. Not only have I been seeing him baby sister, I've been lying to him. A lie by omission is still a lie.

"Because of her brother?"

"Yeah. I don't want to screw up our friendship. But she means a lot to me. And then there's the fact that she's probably going back to England soon. And I live here."

"Why?"

"Why what?" I ask, turning to look at him.

"Why do you have to live here? The B&B will be up and running, your place in Alabama is just a rental. You're between jobs. Nothing stopping you from following her to the UK," he points out and I look over at her again.

"Alex is going to kill me." I groan, putting my head in my free hand. We need to tell him, I know we do. But I want to enjoy our little slice of heaven for as long as I can before reality screws it up.

"You're not the first guy to fall for his best mate's sister, and you sure as hell won't be the last."

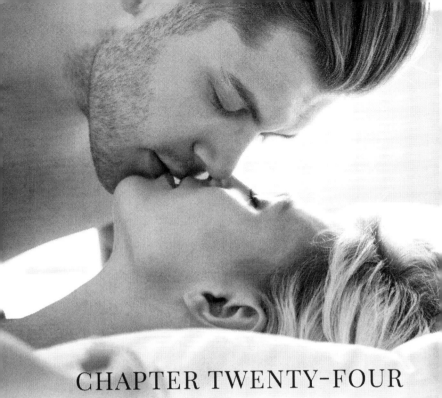

CHAPTER TWENTY-FOUR

Charlotte

Emptying the dishwasher, I hum along to the country song playing on the radio. Putting the clean plates and cutlery in their rightful places, I dance around the kitchen like no one is watching.

Ollie set off early this morning to sort out his rental property he has in Alabama. His landlord lives a few hours from here, and they're meeting up to discuss ending the lease early. He's going to stay here while the place gets up and running, and figure out the rest later. So I busy myself with tidying the house up, texting Ollie a few items we need from the store on his way back.

The knock at the door pulls me from my dance and I turn the radio off, before making my way to the front door. Pulling it open, I smile at the stranger in front of me. Wearing some sort of black messenger bag and pushing his glasses up his nose, he looks out of place.

"Can I help you?" I politely ask, while trying to figure out who he is. We aren't open for business yet, so we aren't expecting visitors.

"Charlotte Maxwell?" he asks.

"Yes?" Uneasiness settles itself in the pit of my stomach, and I feel as if time is slowing down around me.

He pulls a voice recorder out of his back pocket and clicks it on. I feel the colour drain from my face at the realisation of what is happening.

"Michael Anderson, with the *NC Times*. Are you starting a new life here now that your ex-boyfriend is getting married? Do you have any words for the couple before their big day tomorrow?"

"What...?" I try to swallow down the nausea and stay standing, but it isn't easy. Why is this happening? Why do they still care about my car crash of a love life?

"Are you still upset about how publicly you found out about your ex-boyfriend's double life?" First I feel the same wave of panic wash over me. Taking my breath away and causing me to heat all over. But that quickly switches to anger. How dare this man come here, to my safe place, and bring up all those awful memories.

"How did you get this address?" I ask, trying to remain

calm. He has no right to come here and burst my bubble.

He shrugs like it is no big deal, "Someone called my office and told me you were here. Said their name was Oliver, they didn't mind me sharing it, said it wasn't a secret."

And just like that, the heat engulfs me. I slam the door in the reporter's face and lean against it, breathing heavily. The dredged up memory of my public humiliation was upsetting. But Oliver was right, it's in the past and I've moved past it. But knowing that the one man who brought me back to life has betrayed my trust? That is heart-wrenching. How dare he? Why would he do that to me after everything we shared?

Then it hits me. The conversation we had a couple of weeks back. He's trying to get the B&B's name out there, and he said himself, no publicity is bad publicity. He must have been rubbing his hands in glee when he realised he could get a story in the local paper with a mention of this place.

Choking back the tears that are now flowing freely, I run up the stairs and start to pack my things. I can't believe it's ending like this. That it is ending at all. I thought we had something special.

Picking up my phone, I dial my brother's number and let out a relieved sigh when he answers.

"Hey, sis! Are you—"

"Can you book me on the next flight back home please?" I sob down the phone line, wiping my nose with the back of my hand and not caring how disgusting it is.

"Yes, of course. What's happened?" he asks, moving around probably trying to find his laptop.

"I'll explain it all when I get home. Just please, can you get me home?" I ask, my eyes streaming, my voice catching and my heart breaking.

How ironic that the man I thought had put me back together is actually the one who has truly shattered me into pieces.

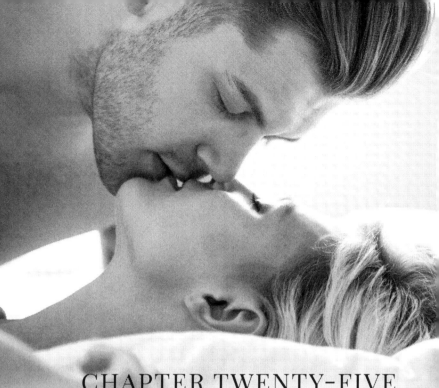

CHAPTER TWENTY-FIVE

Ollie

"**H**oney' I'm home," I singsong into the hallway as I close the front door, dropping the bags of shopping by the door. Silence greets me, and I scrunch my brows in confusion.

Checking the kitchen and lounge to no avail, I head upstairs to look for Charlotte.

"Charlotte?" I call, heading to our room, but she's not there. Just as I turn to leave, I notice her bedside table is empty. Her kindle and perfume are gone. Glancing around the rest of the room, a sinking feeling settles in my stomach. Nothing of hers is here. Moving to the en suite, I'm met with the same sight. A complete lack of anything belonging to her.

Jogging over to the guest room, where her clothes were hanging in the closet, I find it empty.

What the fuck?

Reaching into my jeans pocket, I pull out my phone and dial her number, but it goes straight to voicemail.

"Hey, it's me, call me as soon as you get this, okay?" My voice sounds panicked and breathless but I don't care.

Sitting on the guest bed, I run a hand through my hair in confusion. Where the hell is she? Has something happened?

Scrolling through my phone, I find her brother's number and click call. It rings a couple of times before it stops. Looking down at my phone in confusion, I try again. This time it goes straight to voicemail.

He's avoiding my calls. Did Charlotte tell him about us? Is that what's happened? She let it slip and he's mad? But then why did she pack up and leave? Does she regret what happened between us? Did he make her choose between the two of us and she chose him?

Throwing myself back on the bed, I rub my eyes and think.

How can everything go from being perfect to fucked all in the space of an afternoon?

My phone vibrates beside me and I grab it hoping it's Charlotte but it's not. It's Scott.

"Hey." I sigh heavily.

"Woah, what's up man?" he asks.

"I have no idea. Just got back to the house and Charlotte is gone, as are all of her things. Her phone is going to voicemail, and I can't get through to Alex either."

"Fuck. You think she told him?" he asks and I sit up, rubbing a hand over my face and thinking.

"I guess so. Maybe she accidentally told him and he lost his shit and she panicked and left? I don't know. I would have thought she would have spoken to me first. It's not like her." None of this makes sense. Everything was fine this morning.

"So, what's your plan?"

"What do you mean?"

"Well sitting there moping isn't going to win your woman back. So what is?"

He's right. I can't sit here and do nothing. Alex may not approve of us, but I've been happier these last few weeks with Charlotte than I ever have been before. And I'm not willing to let that go without a fight. Not unless she can look me in the eye and tell me she doesn't feel the same.

"I'm going to England," I say, standing up and making my way to my room.

"Damn right you are. Book a flight and go get your girl."

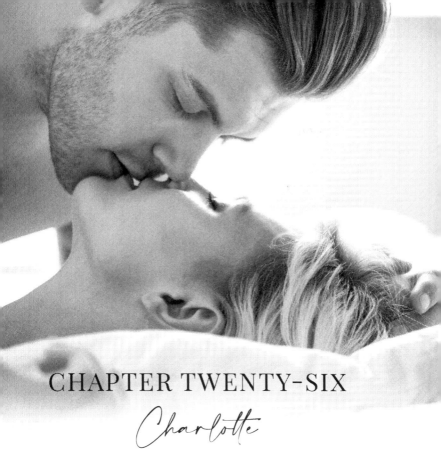

CHAPTER TWENTY-SIX

Charlotte

Arriving at the airport, I feel numb. I spent most of the flight crying, berating myself for trusting again so easily. After pulling my case off of the luggage carousel, I wheel it into arrivals and spot my mum. Tears begin to fall again as I power walk towards her, throwing myself into her open arms.

"It's going to be ok, love," she whispers, rubbing my back to comfort me. Alex must have called her and filled her in. "Let's get out of here and we can talk, okay?"

Nodding, I wipe my eyes with the sleeve of my cardigan and follow her as she wheels my case to the car park, stopping to pay for her ticket.

Once we pull out of the car park, she heads to a drive thru coffee shop and orders us both a coconut latte with a salted caramel shot. I smile at the gesture and gratefully accept mine, trying to ignore the memory of Ollie doing something similar when I first arrived over there.

"Do you want to talk about it?" she asks as she pulls back onto the motorway.

"I don't know what there is to say. I let myself believe he cared about me, that he was different than Carl. But he broke my heart just the same," I choke out, closing my eyes and leaning my head back against the headrest. "But it felt worse this time. Carl hurt me, but looking back I think it was more embarrassment and anger. But with Ollie, I loved him, Mum. God, I'm so stupid! I never learn."

"Don't do that. Don't blame yourself for wanting to see the good in people. That's one of the things I admire about you, you always see the best in everything. It isn't a weakness. It's a strength. And if people take advantage of that, that's on them, Charlotte. Not on you." She puts her hand on mine and I clasp it, so glad I have her.

Taking a sip of my latte, I look out the window and digest what she said.

"I thought he felt the same, but in the end the business was more important. He wanted that to work more than he wanted us to work," my voice breaks again and I shake my head, sick of crying over men.

"Then he's a fool. He knocked you down, but he won't

knock you out. You get back up, put a smile back on your face, and show him what a fool he was to let you go. You're my daughter. The strongest woman I know. Don't let him have the power to break you. Only you have that."

A smile slips onto my face, for the first time in a while and I turn to the woman who is always there for me, no matter what. "I missed you."

"Of course you did, I'm fabulous," she jokes and I laugh and squeeze her hand.

"You're something, alright."

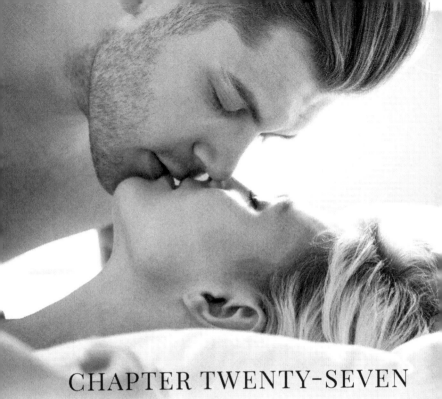

CHAPTER TWENTY-SEVEN

Ollie

Banging on the door like a man possessed, I wait for my best friend to open it. If anyone knows where I can find Charlotte, it's him.

The door opens and his face appears. It goes from neutral to furious in record timing. His eyes narrow and his jaw ticks, fisting his hands to stop himself from lashing out.

"You've got some bloody nerve coming here. I trusted you! I trusted you to look after her, you arsehole!" He's in my face, pushing his finger into my chest and I take it. I crossed a line by pursuing his sister, I know that. He's one of my best friends and I should have known his sister was off limits, I *did* know, but I pursued her anyway.

"I did," I say, frustrated and tired, the long flight catching up with me. I just want to find Charlotte. I understand that he's not thrilled about me and his sister, but he needs to get over it, I'm not going anywhere.

"Yeah? Is that what you call contacting a local reporter and letting them know she was staying with you?" He scoffs, folding his arms across his chest and shooting daggers at me through his glare.

"What? I didn't..." *What the hell?* A reporter found her? How is that possible?

"Save it for someone who cares," Alex spits out as he goes to close the door on me. I slam my hand on the door to keep it from shutting. I need to know what the hell is going on.

"Wait! Alex, I swear to you, I didn't contact a reporter. I wouldn't do that to her." Fuck. Is that what Charlotte thinks? Is that why she ran?

"No? Then why did the reporter tell her that their contact was called Oliver? Explain that."

"What? That's impossible, I would never... *Fuck*, she wouldn't..." The pieces start to fall into place and it feels like time slows down. The events of the last few weeks begin playing on a loop through my mind.

"Who wouldn't?" he growls at me, his face red with anger. He's barely holding it together and I'm actually impressed he's yet to take a swing at me. I deserve it.

"Becky, my ex. She came by a few weeks ago, saw

Charlotte at the house. Wanted to get back together once she saw the house and the money it could make her. Her last name is Oliver, remember? Becky Oliver. You used to joke that I should take her last name if we got married. 'Ollie Oliver, so good they named him twice.'"

"Fuck," Alex curses, rubbing a hand over his tired face. He pulls the door open wider and motions for me to follow him in.

That's progress. At least he isn't shutting me out.

"Christ, I knew she'd do anything for money, but this is low. Even for her." You think you know a person and they do something like this.

"Best thing you ever did was kick her to the curb." Alex nods, rolling his eyes at my poor choice in partner.

"No. The best thing I ever did was fall in love with your sister."

His head snaps up as his eyes meet mine in shock. I hold his stare, not backing down. He needs to know I'm in this for the long haul.

"You love her?"

"More than life itself. I would never do anything to hurt her, Alex. Never. She means the world to me." She's my ocean.

"Seriously, man. I told you to take care of her, not fall for her," he jokes, shaking his head at me. I'm relieved he isn't trying to hit me.

"She made it too hard not to. She's an incredible woman." And she is. I know she thinks she's weak and afraid of the world, but she still gets up every day and lives. She's the bravest person I've ever met.

"You've got it bad."

"You have *no* idea. Now will you help me win her back?"

"You swear to me that you'll never hurt her? She's been through hell, man."

"You have my word. She means everything to me." And she does. Now that I've found her, I can't lose her. The world makes sense when she's with me.

He nods, approving of my answer. "Then let's go get your woman!"

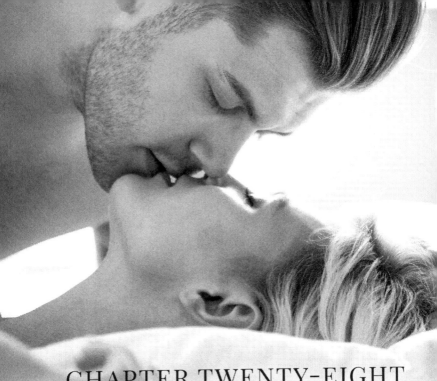

CHAPTER TWENTY-EIGHT

Charlotte

When Mum suggested a weekend away, just us two, I jumped at the chance. I need a break from everything. I thought I'd found where I was meant to be. My safe place. My confidant. But no, all he cared about was getting publicity for his B&B.

Mum's popped down to the spa for her massage. I didn't feel like one just yet so I'm currently curled up on the king-size bed in our hotel room reading a romance novel. With a cup of coffee and a great book, I can pretend for now that my life isn't falling to pieces... again.

It's not even that the video came back to haunt me again. Ollie was right. So what if people see it? It says more about the type of man my ex is than anything. It was one snapshot into my life. One moment. It doesn't define me, and anyone who truly knows me won't judge me by it. No, what is breaking me apart is that the man I fell in love with, the one I trusted to never hurt me. He betrayed my trust for a payday. That's what is breaking my heart and making it hard to breathe.

Alex always mocks me for my love of romance novels, but at least you know what you're getting with them. Ninety-five percent of the time you can guarantee you'll get a happily ever after that makes your heart happy. So here I am, ignoring my train wreck of a story to get lost in someone else's.

A knock at the door pulls me back to reality. Mum must have forgotten her room key. Dropping my book onto the bed, I jump off and make my way to the door. Only when I pull it open, it's not Mum. It's Alex.

"Alex? What are you doing here? Is everything ok?" I ask, confused by his sudden appearance at our girls' retreat.

"Yes, everything is fine, Lottie. I need you to hear this out, ok?" he asks, walking into the room and standing by the bed.

"What's going on?" He's starting to scare me. "Is it Dad? Has something happened?"

"No, everyone's fine. Just trust me, ok?" he says, with a smile and a reassuring squeeze to my hand, then he turns and walks back to the door.

What the hell is happening? Just as I'm about to ask him what is going on, I see him.

Ollie.

With his dark hair and bright green eyes, he looks heart-stoppingly beautiful, even with the look of fatigue on his face. My heart hurts at the sight of him. At the memory of what he did to me. To us.

"What... what are you doing here?" I ask, willing my voice to sound strong but knowing it came out breathless and pained.

"I've been trying to find you," he answers like it's the most obvious answer in the world.

"Ever think that maybe I didn't want to be found?" I ask, annoyed that he has had the nerve to show up and ruin my weekend away with my mum.

"Hear him out, Lot. I'll be down in the hotel bar if you need me," Alex says before leaving and shutting the door behind him. My eyes find Ollie's again and I lose it. I'm not sad anymore. I'm angry. How dare he do this to me, to us.

"You need to leave. Now," I say, turning my back and moving to retrieve my book from where I threw it on the bed.

"Not until you hear me out," he replies and I bristle. Spinning on my heels, I meet his gaze.

"Hear you out? Are you serious? I think you said enough to your reporter friend. I'm curious though. Did it work? Did the publicity help you make bookings for Ocean Dreams? Was it worth it?" I don't realise I'm crying until the tears hit my chest. Angrily, I wipe them away, annoyed that he can see how much he has affected me.

"I didn't, sweetheart. I would never." He steps forward and I hold up a hand to stop him, I can't let him touch me right now.

"Please! The guy told me you were his source. And you said it yourself! No such thing as bad publicity, remember? Anything to get the B&B's name out there!"

"No. Charlotte, I didn't call the reporter. I would never do that to you, and you know that." His eyes pierce my soul, the pain and emotion in them moulding with my own.

"Do I?" I'm shouting now, but I can't help it. All the anger, the hurt, the humiliation, it all comes spilling out like the plug has been pulled. "You told me I could trust you. You made me feel like you actually cared about me. And then you took it all away with one phone call. Why?"

He shakes his head and moves toward me, grabbing my chin and tilting my head to look at him.

"I didn't call that reporter, Charlotte. Hell, I didn't know one had showed up until I spoke to Alex. He said that the guy told you his source was Oliver, right?" I nod, confused as to where this is going.

"My money grabbing ex, her name is Becky Oliver. The one who came over a few weeks ago, remember? My guess is that she saw the video on social media and figured she'd found a way to make an easy buck. Selfish bitch."

What? It wasn't him? But...

"But..."

"I'm crazy about you, Charlotte. You are the best thing that has ever happened to me. You're the sunrise on a quiet morning, the first sip of coffee at the beginning of the day, the bright star that lights up a moonless night. You're everything I ever wanted, but never thought I could have. You make me want to be a better man. I'm hopelessly in love with you and I need you to know, even if you don't feel the same, I need you to know that I would never betray your trust like that."

I feel like the wind has been knocked out of me.

It wasn't him.

He loves me.

"Say something, sweetheart," he begs, running his free hand through his messy hair.

"I love you too," I whisper. The smile that materialises on his face lights up the room and has me smiling back through my tears.

"Yeah?" he asks, almost surprised, which is ridiculous. How could he doubt how strong my feelings are for him?

"Yeah." I laugh. "These past few months I've been the happiest I've ever been, and that's because of you. You showed me that you don't have to be perfect, you just have to be present. And that's what I want to do. I want to live in the present. With you."

"You are perfect, perfect for me."

He leans in and our lips connect. I've missed the taste of him. The feel of his soft lips pressed to mine. Wrapping my arms around his neck, I pull him closer and push up to my tiptoes to get as close to him as humanly possible. As he deepens the kiss, I moan into his mouth, the feel of his tongue dancing with mine sets me on fire. This man knows me better than I know myself.

Moving one hand down to feel his insanely sculpted abs, I try to push his t-shirt up to get better access. Only to be interrupted by the opening of the door.

"Oh, Ollie. What a lovely surprise! Are you staying for tea?"

Pulling back, I hear Ollie chuckle. Cock-blocked by my mother.

Wonderful.

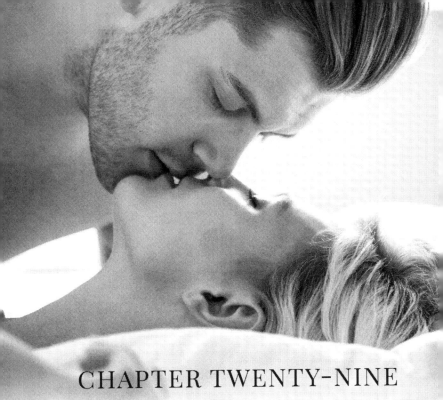

CHAPTER TWENTY-NINE

Ollie

After catching up with Charlotte's mum, I went down to reception and booked a room for the night. We agreed to have dinner together, the four of us, in the hotel restaurant. Then Alex was going to head home, and Charlotte was going to spend the night with me. Her mum insisted she didn't mind spending the night alone, apparently she considered it a treat to get a night without her husband snoring like an angry bear next to her.

Once we've said our goodbyes, I lead Charlotte to the

elevator and push the button for our floor. As the doors close I turn to her. "You ok?"

"Yes, I'm good. Amazing, actually. I feel like a weight has been lifted off of my chest and I can breathe freely for the first time in ages," she admits with a smile. The doors open and I follow her to our room. Putting the key card in, I motion for her to enter first.

"How do you mean?" I ask, carrying on our conversation from the elevator.

"Like, I hit rock bottom. With the whole video thing and then thinking you betrayed my trust. But I'm still here. I'm still going. I guess I feel like the events of the past year have shown me that I'm stronger than I thought. I can weather any storm that comes my way, as long as I take it one step at a time."

Smiling, I pull her into my arms and kiss her on her forehead. She melts into my embrace and I feel like I'm finally home.

"I'm so proud of you, you know that right?" I ask, twirling a loose strand of her blonde hair around my finger.

"What for?" She looks up at me.

"For being this strong, courageous woman. For facing your fears and rising above them. For knowing you deserve better than a liar or a cheat and walking away from me when you thought I had betrayed you, because you knew you deserved better. You've come so far from that coffee snob I picked up from the airport."

She laughs and I cup her cheek. Looking into her ocean blue eyes, I realise that Gram was right. The ocean does heal. Because this beautiful woman, with eyes the colour of the ocean, and hair the colour of the sand, has healed me completely.

"I love you," I whisper into her lips as I claim them. She moans into my mouth and follows my lead. I will never get enough of this woman. Slowly, I lead us to the bed and push her down onto it. Pulling my t-shirt over my head, I watch as her eyes fill with desire. She smiles as she sits up and pulls her dress over her head, throwing it onto the floor and lying back. Climbing up next to her, I lean down and cover her with kisses. Charlotte deserves to be worshipped, and I vow to spend every day doing just that.

Slipping a hand behind her, I unclip her bra and pull the straps down her arms, before letting it join her dress on the floor. Taking a nipple in my mouth, I suck hard and smile at the moan she elicits. I love how she loses her inhibitions in the bedroom. She's not anxious about anything or anyone, she's just pure, unadulterated Charlotte.

"Please," she begs, and I smile against her breast.

"Please what?" I ask, licking my way back up to her face and planting a kiss on her collarbone.

"Please get naked," she pants and I chuckle.

"Anything for you, sweetheart." Pulling back, I stand and unfasten my jeans. Her eyes follow my every movement and fuck, it's one hell of a turn on. To know I affect her as much as she does me.

Pushing both my pants and briefs down, I climb back onto the bed and kiss my way up her body. The soft moans she emits are almost my undoing.

This is where I belong.

EPILOGUE

Charlotte

S itting on the porch, watching the sunrise, I'm still blown away by this view. The waves lap against the shore, dissolving into foam on the soft sand. The soothing sound has me smiling into my coffee. The mix of the oranges and pinks from the sun and the blues and greens of the ocean are stunning, making me wish I were an artist and could capture it in a painting.

The front door creaks open and I turn to see Ollie walk out, shirtless in a pair of loose-fitting jeans. Suddenly the view of the rising sun doesn't seem so impressive.

"Morning, beautiful," he says, his voice still heavy with sleep, and I bite my lip. His eyes darken and I blush, turning back to the view of the ocean. His rough chuckle has the hair on the back of neck standing to attention.

"Morning." It's been two months since he flew over to England to find me. Two months of getting to know each other better, date nights, and getting the B&B ready to open next week. We're already fully booked for the next month, and I couldn't be happier.

"You're up early." He drops a kiss on my head and leans against the railing, looking out to the ocean. My eyes make their way from his back to his jeans. I still can't believe this is real. That we're real. These past eight weeks have been nothing short of magic.

Standing, I make my way over to him and wrap my arms around him, placing a soft kiss on his back. He turns with a sinful smile and cups my cheek, causing sparks to shoot through me. His touch never fails to set me alight, his gaze always penetrates my soul. Every part of me was made for every part of him. Leaning forward, he kisses me like he always does, like he can't believe I'm real. And I know the feeling.

Wrapping my arms around his neck, I pull him closer, moaning into his mouth when his tongue touches mine. Desire spreads through every part of me, and I want to lose myself in him.

With a tortured groan, he pulls back. "Let's not start something we can't finish, sweetheart. Melody and Scott will be here soon."

He's right, I know he is, but I still pout and bury my head into his chest. His deep chuckle makes my head bounce and I lightly smack him so he stops.

"I'll never get over this view," he says, his voice filled with wonder and I turn to look out to the ocean.

"I know, it's something else."

"I feel like it's my duty to make sure everyone knows how beautiful it is, to get people to come here and find themselves and make memories. How lame is that?"

"It isn't lame, it's beautiful," I say, smiling up at him. "Tell you what, why don't we start spreading the word now?"

He looks at me in confusion, not sure where I'm going with this and I smile and pull back. Grabbing my phone from the table, I pull up the camera and put it on selfie mode before handing it to him.

"Let's take a selfie for the B&B's social media, show the world why they need to visit."

If you'd told me a couple of months ago I'd be uploading my life for all to comment on again, I'd have laughed in your face. But right here, in this moment, there is nothing I want more than to capture this perfect moment with this perfect man. To shout from the rooftops that he's mine.

"Yeah?" he asks, knowing what a big step this is for me. But I'm done letting the past dictate my future. You only get one life, and I'm going to enjoy every moment of mine.

Nodding, I snuggle into his side, smiling as he brings the camera up to get both of us and the beach in the picture.

"Smile," he says, and I do.

I never stop.

ACKNOWLEDGMENTS

To my wonderful friends Sybil and Becca. I am forever grateful for all of your support and encouragement. You have no idea how much I treasure your friendship.

To my family. For being my biggest supporters and such a great sounding board. Special shout out to Mum and Nan for reading all my books, even if they make you blush.

To Alex – Thank you for being you. Your graphics, teasers, and words of encouragement are appreciated more than you know. Our random conversations, gif wars, rants, and daily rambles make me smile. I have no idea how I got so lucky to have you as a friend, but I'm afraid you're now stuck with me forevermore. Sorry, not sorry.

To Lou at LJDesigns. Thank you for another wonderful cover, formatting that never ceases to blow my mind, and for being a wonderful friend. And special shout out to Jax and Opie! Love you guys.

To Beth at Magnolia Author Services. Thank you for making my words shine. You're a joy to work with.

To my reader group. You guys rock! I'm beyond grateful for your support.

Another huge thank you to my wonderful husband. You make me laugh every day, put up with the crazy hours I spend writing, and always support me. I love you more than coffee.

And as always, to my baby. I love you so much. Thank you for making me smile every day.

Thank you for reading! I really appreciate you taking

the time to read my words. If you wouldn't mind leaving a review, I would be eternally grateful!

BOOKS BY SOPHIE BLUE

What Are You Weighting For? Series

Weighting On Love

Fighting For Love

Running From Love

The Carrington Brothers Series

Blindsided By The Billionaire

Standalones

Meet Me In The Sunflowers

Co-Writes with Alexandra Silva

Love 2 Jingle U

Love 2 Hate U

N2HU

ABOUT THE AUTHOR

Sophie Blue is a hopeless romantic and avid reader. She fell in love with reading at a young age and can always be found with her nose in a book. She started writing after having her baby and published her debut rom com in May 2020.

A coffee addict and HEA lover, Sophie lives just outside of London with her husband and mini me. She writes contemporary romance filled with fun, sweet feels.

www.sophieblueauthor.com

Stay in touch!

facebook.com/sophieblueauthor
instagram.com/SophieBlueAuthor
twitter.com/SophieBlueAuth
amazon.com/author/sophieblue
bookbub.com/profile/sophie-blue
goodreads.com/SophieBlue-Author

SOPHIE
BLUE
Coffee, Kisses and Endless Wishes

Printed in Great Britain
by Amazon